About the Author

Lucineh is an author of Armenian descent and French and British nationality, born and raised in London. Lucineh holds a bachelor's and a master's degree and has been an educator for over a decade. Writing has always been a strong passion of hers and has played a key role in shaping her professional and personal life's journey. When writing, Lucineh chooses to live vicariously through each character in order to best tell their story with the authenticity that each one deserves. Lucineh has a strong interest in literature, languages and culture and hopes to inspire her readers through her work.

Lost Souls

Love,

Lucineh

x

Lucineh Danielian

Lost Souls

Olympia Publishers
London

www.olympiapublishers.com
OLYMPIA PAPERBACK EDITION

A CIP catalogue record for this title is
available from the British Library.

ISBN: 978-1-80439-646-9

This is a work of fiction.
Names, characters, places and incidents originate from the writer's
imagination. Any resemblance to actual persons, living or dead, is
purely coincidental.

First Published in 2024

Olympia Publishers
Tallis House
2 Tallis Street
London
EC4Y 0AB

Printed in Great Britain

Dedication

This collection of short stories is dedicated to my beloved grandmother, Alice Dilanian, born Sarafian, forever loved and cherished. *Pour toi, douce mamie.*

A Note to Readers

Dear Readers,

You are preparing to meet six unique females you have not yet encountered, each unknowingly in a search for truth and identity.

Yet ask yourselves, what is identity? A simple word, yet one which is complex and should be profoundly reflected upon.

Do we define our own identity? Or does identity define us? Are we masters of our own selves or is our identity predetermined in some way?

Shaping one's identity is a lifelong journey. A journey that is challenging, thought-provoking, a struggle at times, yet a worthwhile, insightful and valuable lesson of life.

Readers, as you delve into each story, accompany these women in their quest for identity and embark on this journey with them. Help them to determine their place in the world and find their voice.

Remember, readers, *you* have a voice. You are the voice of truth.

Nobody Noticed

What do you do when you feel the person that you love disappoints you? Not in the usual way. Not just any kind of disappointment. The deep kind. The kind that stings. Really stings. In fact, it stings so deep, you don't dare even go there. If you do, it will only hurt more.

Is that what she was afraid of? Of getting hurt? Really getting hurt? Time is a great healer, isn't it? It's time that helps to bring perspective and time that heals you slowly but surely, or at least that's what they say.

Yet what if the person who disappoints you, the person who opens that wound, the person who stops protecting you just when you need protecting the most is the person that you would give your life for, the person that you love more than anything or anyone in the world, the person that you have grown up with, admired, learnt from. What if you are so disappointed and hurt, you just don't feel that you can go back? What do you do then?

Do you confront them yet again and try to make them see your side? Hang on, haven't you done that countless times? Aren't you tired of searching for that approval, knowing deep down there's a chance you will never get it? Or do you grieve? Do you grieve a bond you thought you had, knowing that it has been harmed? Knowing that you will never get the approval you are searching for or feel that you deserve?

Where does approval even come from? And why as children do we crave it so much? And why then as adults, does that craving increase? Why aren't we able to cut the cord? Why do we keep trying to be the martyrs we are not meant to be?

So many questions, yet so few answers... So little time, yet so much of it consumed by negativity and fear.

What if we were to start living, truly living? What if we were to wake up one day and find out what life would be like without needing someone else to tell us that everything will be OK, that we are good people, and that our life choices are the right ones? What if...?

As a young child, Lauren had searched so deeply for this approval. She had begged for it, pleaded at times. She had even been on her knees. Yet no matter how much she did for her parents, it was never enough. It never felt like enough. And yet, she just kept trying.

She would leave the tap on and let the sink overflow in the hope that her parents would notice she needed them. Oh, they noticed. They noticed their wet floor. They noticed the dripping ceiling. And boy did they scream. They screamed the house down. They screamed so loud, the neighbours knocked to check on the situation.

She was ready to admit she hadn't thought that one through. All she wanted was a little love, a hug here and there. A smile even.

She would sometimes leave the light on, knowing full well her parents were trying to cut down on energy bills. She would leave it on for hours just waiting for one of her parents to check on the situation. And they did. Oh, how they did. How they yelled. They yelled at her irresponsible attitude, her careless behaviour and her nasty streak.

Yet she hadn't banked on this. She hadn't banked on this reaction. All she wanted was to be noticed. Just once. She was three, for God's sake.

So, she kept on. She would leave the fridge door open. She would leave the tap running, Fairy liquid dripping into the sink. She would leave her shoes in the way, knowing someone could trip at any moment. She would even leave the back door open on the odd occasion, knowing full well the neighbour's dog would invite itself in. *Oops*, she thought…

How many times did she get asked why she acted this way? Why she did such things? Why she was so careless? And still nobody caught on. And then she realised this really was the only way to get noticed. Nothing was ever going to change. Her parents were never going to actually love her. But she would get noticed. It got to the point where any kind of attention would do. Something was better than nothing.

The problem was, the older she got, the more imaginative and creative she became. Why invest your energy in school when you can spend your time winding people up, just for the sake of it? Forget school. That was never going to get Lauren anywhere. It's not like anyone ever noticed or read her report cards.

There was one year when she really had tried. It was the year she had taught herself to read. She and only she had helped herself. The teacher and assistant at school were useless. They would look at her like some invalid. What was the point of phonics? No, no, she wanted to get to the good stuff. That's where all the words were.

Every day, without anyone noticing, she would put a book in her bag. You weren't supposed to take books home. You weren't even supposed to touch the school books unless you were carefully assisted.

She waited till the moment the milk came out. Milk and fruit.

God, was that what life was about when you were four? Milk and fruit? No thank you! Not when you could be shopping in the library corner at school without anyone noticing. And so she learnt to pick up a book, quietly slide it into her bag, and slip back into her seat. She managed to get away with that for a whole year.

She couldn't help sometimes pretending she couldn't read. She would sit there watching these idiots mouth random syllables. God forbid they read a word to her. Oh no! Not a full word. Lauren would sit there, on that magic carpet and watch them.

One day, she got tired of that game. She decided to show them what she could do. So she did it. She picked up a book, stood up and read a word. She could feel all eyes were on her. She had definitely been noticed that day.

The school had contacted her mum and dad. They were probably at work at the time and couldn't pick up. There was no other explanation. Surely if this wasn't the case, they would say something. Surely, they would notice that their little five-year-old could read!

Except it was the case, wasn't it. She found this out as she picked up the school letter that had been scrunched up and carelessly thrown in the bin.

That day, she learnt a harsh lesson. The harshest lesson of all. That's the moment she stopped stealing books. She sat at the table just like every other kid in her class, waiting for that one piece of fruit and that small glass of milk.

She hated fruit. She hated milk. She hated life.

She had to face facts. Nobody actually cared. Nobody was going to start caring just because she willed it to happen. It wasn't going to happen. The sooner she understood that, the sooner she could get on with her life. She knew how to read now. That was something. Writing didn't seem like such a task either. She would perfect that skill in no time. Just imagine how much she could do then. The stunts she could pull without getting noticed. It didn't matter that she was five. If anything, the earlier the better. The earlier she could start to get on with her life, the closer she would be to freedom.

She had to think of a plan. She had to think about the next few years and find a strategy. And in the meantime, that attention she was so used to getting could keep her entertained. With every parent, there's a pattern, and once you can figure out the pattern, you can figure out the game. And if you can figure out the game, there's nothing left to be afraid of.

She didn't care that her dad was starting to miss important calls. *Oops*, she didn't mean to unplug the phone. She would plug it back in soon enough and nobody would be any the wiser. Look, if he didn't want anyone messing with his system, he shouldn't leave his work diary lying there. Reading really did come in handy. Ha! And the trick was to stay one step ahead. One step ahead of the game and one step ahead of the two people that hated having her around.

Was it really her problem that after a while, clients stopped calling? Did she really worry that his insurance company was going downhill? Sure, she read the notices. After all, she could read. But they meant nothing to her. She had stopped caring the day she realised nobody else cared.

Nor did she care that some of those final notices were going missing. *Oops*! She didn't think anyone would notice anyway. And even if they did, how would they ever figure out who the culprit was?

While that was going on, Lauren was too busy to notice what was happening to her dad. She was too busy multitasking, too busy changing the time on the alarm clock. Too busy in fact making sure her mum no longer made it to work on time. It served her right. How dare she not once think of walking Lauren to school! How dare she forget to sign the trip form to the aquarium. And how dare she forget to wash Lauren's uniform.

After a while, she stopped getting screamed at. She stopped getting yelled at. In fact, she stopped getting spoken to altogether. There really wasn't much left to say. Her dad had once thrown away the most precious piece of paper she had ever been the proud owner of and so she had done exactly the same to him. Tit for tat.

It was often tit for tat in her family. Lauren would often watch her mum punish her dad the exact same way he punished her. That's what they did. That is, until the business went bust and her dad went bankrupt. Things started to change then. Lauren was eight.

Lauren failed to notice the night her dad didn't come home. She just assumed he was getting away from his wife and child. That's what he always said he wanted to do. Whenever he argued with his wife, her mother that is, he would threaten to leave and walk out on them. They would both get into a steaming row, which would result in her mum running after her dad, getting on her knees if she had to. In those moments, the family wouldn't go unnoticed. In fact, they'd be the talk of the town and Lauren would have to hear all about it at school. Walking down the corridor would be a nightmare sometimes. An absolute nightmare. Home time wouldn't be a barrel of laughs either. The same little group of busy bodies would be discussing her family's shenanigans, as they waited to pick up their children. That's how she spent the rest of her primary school years, right up to year seven.

She'd sit in class sometimes listening in on others' conversations and questions about the maths homework or the English creative writing piece. She never actually did these anymore. What was the point? It's not as if anyone actually gave a damn. Yes, a few phone calls had been made and a few letters had been sent home but nobody actually followed up on any of this. Funny how the phone was disconnected most of the time so nobody could get through. Was a message left on the answering machine? Well, not anymore! And as for the letters, well, they were in the bin along with the rubbish, just where they belonged.

Truancy was the big thing at her school. If a child didn't come to school, then teachers would start running around like headless chickens. That is when her mum at least noticed, not because she cared about the whereabouts of her daughter. Oh no. God forbid. It was all about the fine for her mum. A fine she couldn't afford to pay and a fine that just wasn't worth the hassle for Lauren. *Just go to school and see the days out.*

She figured the fun would come in high school. Year seven would be the year of change.

And then year seven came and Lauren turned twelve. She didn't bank on a period the first day of school. She was not prepared for this eventuality. Nobody had warned her beforehand. She'd read about it and done her homework, knowing full well her mother certainly wouldn't. But she wasn't ready. And besides, she didn't have anyone to share this news with. Her dad was hardly around. He was out boozing most of the time. He was quite the womaniser these days and came and went as he pleased. Her mum was always in bits. She could barely make it to work. Lauren didn't even need to play around with her alarm clock anymore. Her mum was gladly wasting her own time. And while she was doing that, she was too busy to see the blood stains on her daughter's tights. She was too preoccupied to notice the stained sheets Lauren had to sleep in. She didn't have time for her daughter these days. Come to think of it, she hadn't had time for Lauren in a very long time, if ever in fact. But she remained oblivious to this. She had too much on her mind and her husband was all she could think about these days. Where was he? What was he doing? Who was he with? She never got any answers, ever. It's like he didn't even care anymore. It was worse than being invisible, or so she thought.

Lauren started getting noticed at school. She was starting to get in with the crowd. The girls she had once been completely ignored by were now joining her for lunch and the boys who had once laughed at her were busy eyeing her up these days. If she was honest, she quite liked the attention. Never mind that she started to make other people's lives a misery at school, people she had once hung around with. It was all part of the game, all part of getting noticed by the right people. She had trouble feeling anything half the time so she certainly didn't feel bad for any of her actions. If anything, she was numb to them. Lauren never really knew how to take the attention she was given. Let's face it. She was never given that attention by her parents and her parents had never had any other kids. Just as well, seeing as they apparently hated their own. And so if she felt nothing, she put it down to their style of parenting, if you could even call it that.

The more attention she got, the stranger it felt. She wasn't used to being noticed at all, let alone by boys. And the older she got, the more attention she got. She started to enjoy this role and took herself quite seriously. She would steal her mum's makeup almost daily. Her mum was hardly using it these days. She would sometimes take money from her mum's purse. Her mum never even noticed that money was going missing. She was too busy pining after her dad, as her dad was feeding into his midlife crisis. This was the perfect time for Lauren to start getting what she wanted. Other girls envied her freedom which made her feel respected. She had never been respected like this before. Girls looked up to her and boys looked at her. Teachers on the other hand weren't all that impressed, but she didn't have time to waste on what people thought of her. She hadn't before, so why should she start now?

She was fourteen when she got asked to her first party. The parents were away apparently and it was a sort of now or never situation. She couldn't say no. After all, she was the centre of attention. How could she ever say no to this? Other girls wondered how Lauren was always so confident. Lauren didn't see it as confidence. The way she saw it, she was just being herself. And being herself was working for her.

Boy after boy was asking to dance with her. One or two were getting a bit too close for comfort. So when Jack came to check on her, she was relieved. Jack was the most popular boy in school. He didn't even need to bat an eyelid to get people to do things for him. People just did. Everyone was always trying to get Jack's approval. Jack never needed to try. He was who he was and he made no excuses for it. Lauren liked that quality.

They both stood for just a moment, both wondering what to say. It wasn't like them to get all shy. Lauren wasn't shy these days. Jack had certainly never acted this way. She couldn't work it out. For just a moment, Lauren felt like she had him to herself. For just a moment, she felt like she could get closer to him. Really close. She wasn't used to feeling anything. This was new. She didn't quite know how to take the feeling. But before she could even think about it, he was gone. He'd been called away by the cavalry. Lauren stood there, trying to get that feeling back.

She got handed a drink by someone she hardly recognised. She thought he was in her class but then, she didn't really pay too much attention to people who weren't worth her time. She gladly took the drink and didn't question it. God, it tasted strong! A little too strong for her liking. But then that's probably what these parties were all about. As she took her first sip, the lights started to get hazy and Lauren came over all dizzy. She wasn't quite sure what was going on. But before she knew it, she was out of it. And that was it.

Lauren woke up the next morning in a bed she didn't recognise. All she knew was that it wasn't her own. Her heart started pounding. Her head was throbbing. Where the hell was she? Whose bed was this? Whose house was this? Was that the boy who'd given her a drink last night? Was that his face on the wall? She didn't wait to find out.

How did she even get out of there? She was really starting to panic now. She didn't feel like herself at all. In fact, she was about to be sick. Really sick.

She didn't remember how she made it home. But she was home. She had never been so glad to see her bedroom. She checked her phone. Three missed calls. Whoever that was could wait. It was time for a shower and a hot drink.

The next week, she kept her head down at school. She didn't need anyone asking any ridiculous questions. She avoided eye contact as much as she could. She stopped answering calls, stopped searching for unwanted attention, stopped caring about what anyone else thought of her. She wished she could shrink and hide away, as far as life could take her.

Her and Jack crossed paths a few times that week but he didn't say a word to her. Why should he? He had no reason to talk to her. None of the girls in the group were speaking to her either. It was like she didn't exist anymore. And that night at the party was completely fake. Of course it was. A dare of some kind. How stupid she had been to believe that she was ever in with a chance. How ridiculous to think that any other girl ever wanted to be like her, let alone any boy want her. Had she just imagined all that attention? Had she made it up? Or was it just that they were that fake? It didn't matter either way. She had never trusted anyone. She hadn't known what that was like. And if she was honest with herself, she had never felt so alone in her life.

She got home that day to find her mum in bed yet again. That was all her mum ever did these days. She only got dressed on the odd occasion. Her dad hadn't been home in weeks. Not that she knew of anyway. It was up to Lauren to do the washing up, put her mum's clothes away, and clear up the table. Her mum didn't seem to notice anything anymore. She used to pride herself on a clean house. These days, that was the last thing on her mind. Lauren was the last thing on her mind but then, she was the last thing on anyone's mind.

Lauren opened the fridge, in the hope that there was something to eat, anything. Who was she kidding? There never was. It wasn't like anyone got hungry since her dad had decided to start his midlife crisis. Long overdue really. And as for her mum, Lauren had been waiting years for this kind of breakdown. She almost missed the screaming matches. Almost. She missed food even more though.

She went upstairs to let her mum know she was going out. Her mum had a faraway look these days, like she just wasn't present anymore. Lauren probably should've been worried but she had enough to worry about as it was. Every time she shut her eyes since the party, she felt uneasy. She felt like someone was behind her, waiting in the shadows. She didn't dare even think about it. Denial was the way to go right now. Her parents had been so good at it. She had had great teachers growing up. And if they could do it, she could do it better.

She decided to take a walk. She knew the area like the back of her hand. She knew where Jack lived as well. Oh! Why was she going back to that now? Was now really the time? Was there ever a good time to think about these things?

For the first time in a very long time, she wished she could find someone to speak to, anyone who would listen. Well not just anyone, someone though. She needed to feel safe. She never really had, to be honest, but she had never felt this unsafe in the world either. She was alone, and there was nobody to comfort her, tell her everything was going to be OK. *It wasn't but it would be.* For the first time in her life, she longed to hear those very words. She had never heard them before, not when she was growing up. She was still growing up now, but still she was under no illusions things would change.

She didn't realise she had been walking for hours. It was starting to get dark and looking around, she realised she didn't quite know the area. It was time to go back. Time to walk home. God knows how long that would take, but then it wasn't like anyone was waiting for her.

She took a breath and turned around. It took her a second to realise Jack was staring at her from a distance. What was he doing? How long had he been standing there? Was it really him? She froze for a second. There it was again! That feeling. What was that feeling and why did it keep creeping in when he was around?

Slowly, Lauren walked towards Jack. She wasn't sure what to make of this situation and had to admit she wasn't entirely comfortable with it. She was in a state of vulnerability. That night had brought her back to this state and her bubble had burst. Prior to that night, she was relaxed, confident, sure of herself. At least, that's what it had felt like. And now, she was back to being alone, lonely, somehow invisible. Her heart was beating, pounding almost. What was Jack doing there? She couldn't work it out. All she knew was that the attraction she had felt for Jack at the party that night had turned into a feeling of utter fear and she couldn't quite explain what was happening to her.

She knew better than to let her guard down. That's one thing her mum had taught her over the years, never to let your guard down no matter who you're dealing with. Even as a family, it felt like they never had. And she wasn't about to change her ways tonight in the middle of a street she didn't quite recognise with a guy she didn't quite feel like she knew.

It was her birthday tomorrow. Imagine that, another birthday! Fifteen years old and not much to show for it. Anyway, now wasn't the time to reflect on her depressing life and an even more depressing birthday to go with it.

Jack smiled as Lauren approached him. He could obviously see that she was freezing as he handed her his jacket and put his arms around her. She didn't refuse, although her gut was telling her to. She followed his lead and they walked home in silence. With every step, she wondered what he was doing. Why was he there? Should she ask him? She didn't dare. She let herself be dragged home, slowly.

She didn't need to direct him. He seemed to know where she lived. She was too exhausted to ask any questions. She knew that this whole situation was strange in so many ways, but she just didn't have the energy to question it further. So she ignored her gut as they got to the door. She let him drop her off. She let him put his soft lips on hers and gently kiss her good night. She let him put his arms around her one last time before he walked away just as comfortably as he'd walked towards her. Nevertheless, something didn't feel quite right. She didn't feel quite right.

As she got in, she realised the kitchen light had been left on. Her mum was nowhere to be seen. She didn't have the energy to check on the situation. She went straight to her room and turned on the light. And at that point, she realised he had left his jacket with her. A coincidence? Probably. She turned off the light and got into bed, leaving the jacket on the chair.

She fell asleep almost immediately. She found herself at the party again, Jack stood next to her, that same smile on his face. She was handed the drink again a moment later by someone she hardly recognised. The next thing she knew, she was being led upstairs to a room she'd never seen before. She couldn't make out the person's face. She was in a bedroom, being laid onto a bed. Who was there? Who had brought her up and who was getting into bed next to her?

She woke up panting and sweating, terrified of what she had just recollected. What the hell had happened that night? And why was it all such a blur? She was getting really scared now. She curled up in a ball, holding onto her duvet as hard as she possibly could. It took her a while to shut her eyes again, but slowly, she fell back to sleep.

The next morning was tough. She hadn't got much sleep. What's worse, she woke up feeling more alone than ever, not knowing what to do with what she had dreamt or who to turn to.

She got ready for school, had a slice of toast and set off, the jacket in her hand. The scent on it was vaguely familiar. She didn't know where from but she had definitely smelt that scent somewhere. She didn't remember feeling this nauseous previously, but then, she didn't remember much. She set off, confused and alone.

She got to school early enough to look for Jack. She could see him from a distance. He didn't notice she was there. She thought it best to leave it at that. She took his jacket and hung it on his locker. The note read a simple 'Thank you,' though she wasn't feeling very thankful. If anything, she was far from thankful for his actions. She hadn't asked to see him at the party and certainly hadn't expected to be followed. That was after all the only explanation. Her gut was telling her there was something wrong with this whole situation.

English was next, the only subject she liked. It wasn't a bad way to start her fifteenth birthday. A little literature to start the day never hurt anyone! She felt safe in English, protected by words, thoughts and ideas. Ideas and thoughts that were hers and hers alone. Nobody could take them away from her. She sat at the back of the class, hoping she wouldn't be noticed by anyone that way. That was the last thing she needed, especially when she suspected everyone knew about the other night. They probably knew more than she did. They were probably in on it, all those people who had pretended to be her friends.

The bell rang and others started to come in. Nobody approached her. Jack didn't come near her, didn't even bat an eyelid when looking straight at her. Lauren noticed he was wearing his jacket again, the one she'd left on his locker. What was he playing at? What was he trying to achieve?

During the class, she tried really hard to forget about him. She focused all her attention on *Frankenstein*. Lauren had read it three times, which should've given her an advantage, but she just couldn't concentrate long enough to answer any of the questions. Her eyes kept scanning the room. She felt so nervous. She couldn't quite pinpoint what was going on. She couldn't wait for the class to end. All she could think about was the cold indifferent look Jack had given her when walking into the class, like somehow he had a hold over her. And then there was the other night when his gaze couldn't have been more inviting if he'd tried. She wasn't going crazy was she? Not yet. She was way too young to be imagining such scenarios.

Ms Williams, the English teacher, came over looking all worried and concerned. She sent Lauren away to the nurse and wouldn't take no for an answer. Lauren didn't realise how pale she looked, white as a sheet. As she dragged herself out of the class as quietly as possible, she could hear the whispers. They were probably all having a whale of a time gossiping about her. She couldn't worry about that now. She just needed to get away.

She didn't realise how dizzy she felt until she actually left the classroom. Ms Williams followed her out and made sure Lauren got to the nurse's room safely. And as she left Lauren after forcing her to lie on the bed, she walked back out. Lauren could feel the tears streaming down her face at that point. She couldn't stop herself. She must have cried herself to sleep and before she knew it, she felt her eyes shut and the room go totally dark.

Lauren woke up in a sweat. She had obviously been dreaming again, though what that was didn't feel much like a dream, but more like a nightmare. She found herself in that same room, being laid down onto the bed. She could feel someone's presence next to her, but still for the life of her couldn't make out who it was. Whoever they were, she could smell that same familiar scent. Lauren calmed her breathing and after a few moments of panic, she lay her head back down onto the pillow and relaxed.

After that day, Lauren decided to keep her head down. No

more drawing attention to herself. She stayed focused on her school work as much as she could and made herself as invisible as possible. She didn't want a repeat performance of the English class. Nobody needed to see that twice. She was encouraged by the nurse to speak to her parents about what had happened so that they could monitor her more closely. Little did the nurse know that her parents had stopped monitoring her a long time ago. Probably at birth.

Lauren didn't really leave the house anymore. She never even left her room. School and home were her only two journeys each day. She was getting more and more afraid of her own shadow and she didn't dare take any random walks in case she bumped into anyone. Jack was at the top of that list. The less she hung around outside, the less of a chance he had of catching her. If someone had told her a year ago that she would be this afraid of anyone, she would have laughed in their face. But she wasn't laughing now.

Lauren was finding it increasingly difficult to fall asleep. She felt like someone was watching her constantly and she didn't know how to deal with it. She didn't feel like she could talk to anyone. She hardly saw her mum these days. It was hard to believe they even lived under the same roof. As for her dad, he was never around. She couldn't remember the last time she had even seen him, let alone spent any time with him. And let's be honest, they had never been the type of parents to take an interest in Lauren. She had never been asked about her days at school. Her parents had never reminded her to do her homework. They had never even set a curfew. It's like she just didn't exist, like all the family did was to live and breathe the same air, but that was as far as it went. Lauren wasn't about to change this dynamic.

Lauren slept with one eye open. She couldn't quite identify

why or what was keeping her up at night. Maybe it was the darkness that increased the feeling of fear that lived inside her. Or maybe it was that the nights led to her thinking more. There was something in that theory. In fact, all she could remember of that year was the sleepless nights. She tried to throw herself into her education, thinking that one day, if she worked hard enough, she could actually contemplate going to university and getting away from this hell. Every day felt like hell. Every night felt like the same nightmare. And every few days, that same dream would creep back in and overpower her. She would wake up crying, sobbing, screaming some nights. You would think her mum would hear her, but no such luck.

Over the next few months, she attempted to keep up her routine. This way, she could get on with things and try her very best to forget what was going on around her, what was happening to her. She was really trying. Meanwhile, she didn't realise she was hardly eating. She was getting more and more dehydrated. Her body was getting weaker and skin more pale. A good few times, she was late for school. Her energy levels were so low that even getting ready felt like a weight in itself. There was hardly ever anything in the fridge. Was her mum even going shopping? She guessed not.

At school, nobody was speaking to her. Nobody was checking to see if she was doing OK. Nobody but Jack. There he was again, reappearing. He was certainly choosing his moments carefully. God forbid anyone should see him. If she was late to class, she noticed that at times, he would be too. And on those occasions, when going to her locker, she noticed it was slightly ajar. Strange, as she always made sure to lock it. Her essays would often disappear and books borrowed from the library would go missing. She would go home panicking, knowing she wouldn't be handing in her work on time. She was getting detention more and more which just added to the pressure of being at school. Often, Jack would get detention on the same days. How could that be? Was he trying to get punished as well? Or was he just enjoying seeing what was becoming of her?

Often, past the deadline, she would find the book back in her locker. The essays would magically reappear. It was too late to do anything about it. How do you explain to a teacher that things are disappearing and then as if by magic, you find them right back where they were in the first place? Was there any point? Who would believe her? No. These would just be taken as excuses. Excuse after excuse. There was no point in trying to argue her case. There was no case.

The final straw was the day she found a note lying there. It read *'Thanks for the help. You're a star. Got an A+ on the Frankenstein essay. Couldn't have done it without you.'* Before she could help it, she felt the tears running down her face. She looked around her. There he was, acting like butter wouldn't melt, that malicious smile on his face. He stared her straight in the eyes for what felt like hours. She looked away and tried to recompose herself. When she looked back, he was gone.

Lauren was reaching her sixteenth birthday when her English teacher held her back after class. She was getting increasingly concerned. She had left messages with Lauren's parents but surprise, had received no reply. She had sent a good few emails but hadn't got anything back. So she had taken the next step and referred Lauren to the school counsellor. She realised it wasn't ever easy to confide in a stranger, but she never saw Lauren with anyone. She was worried Lauren had nobody to talk to. It was a difficult age and being alone was the last thing Lauren needed.

Lauren stayed quiet throughout the conversation and suppressed any kind of emotion. She accepted Ms Williams' invitation to see the counsellor that afternoon and walked away. She guessed there was no harm in trying, though she had absolutely no idea what she would say or where she would start.

Lauren was quiet at the session. She didn't know where to begin. She didn't trust this woman, nor did she really trust herself these days. She could hear the clock ticking. It felt almost daunting. She thought for a moment about telling the counsellor about the note, but she stopped herself as she looked past the glass door. She couldn't believe her eyes. There he was again. How did he know how to find her? What was he doing standing there?

She could hear the quiet echo of the counsellor's questions that resonated inside her head. She couldn't speak. She could barely even breathe. She had never felt so unsafe in her life. The counsellor took this to mean that Lauren wasn't ready to talk. It was OK to feel worried about opening up. There was no rush, no pressure. They could meet again next week, same time, same place. The session was coming to an end and the counsellor had another student waiting outside.

Lauren stood up without thinking, grabbed her things and ran off. She ran as fast as she could. She ran as fast as her legs would take her. Except they didn't. They didn't take her anywhere. Before she knew it, she had collapsed.

She woke up confused in a room she barely recognised. How had she got here? The nurse came in, relieved to find Lauren awake. A student had come to check on her apparently, a male student. No guesses as to who the nurse was talking about. Surely this wasn't normal behaviour. It couldn't all just be in her head. She couldn't believe he had actually got her doubting herself this much. She was constantly second guessing herself. It had never been this extreme. She couldn't do anything without wondering whether or not she was making the right decision. She couldn't even think without confusing herself. He was inside her head and as much as she wished it, he wasn't going anywhere.

The nurse gave Lauren a bite to eat. She was concerned about Lauren's health. When was the last time Lauren had had something decent to eat? When was the last time Lauren had got a good night's sleep? The nurse should have sent Lauren home early, but when she looked up and saw that Lauren had fallen back to sleep, she just didn't have the heart to wake her up. She waited until she had no choice but to send Lauren home. Believe it or not, this was the first time in months Lauren had actually felt rested.

When Lauren got home, she walked in to find an envelope at the door. It obviously hadn't been posted as there was no stamp or address, just Lauren's name. Lauren could feel her hands shaking. She was dreading what she was about to do. She opened the envelope to find a photograph of herself. It had obviously been taken the night of the party. She recognised the clothes she was wearing. The back read 'Had a great time. Never knew you could be so entertaining. What a memorable night. I hope it was as memorable for you as it was for me.' Was this some kind of sick joke? What the hell was going on? Lauren dropped onto the floor and began to sob uncontrollably. She knew her mum was home, but it was no use. She was alone, unnoticed and alone.

Lauren was breaking down completely. She could feel it. She had no strength left. She had nothing left to give. No reason left to fight. He was obviously getting off on these sick jokes. The mind games were getting unbearable. That night had been the greatest mistake of her life. But how could it be a mistake if she couldn't even remember what had happened? Except she had to be honest with herself. Even if she couldn't quite remember, there was a reason she had blocked it out so well. There was a reason the last thing she remembered was taking a sip of the vodka more than tonic that was handed to her. There was a reason she had woken up wearing the same clothes. She just couldn't bring herself to admit it. She couldn't say it. She couldn't say it and she couldn't tell anyone.

Her mum was the last person she wanted to talk to. She didn't have any friends, none that she could trust. She had always been a loner, even during that short period where she had people to hang out with. They weren't really her friends. They weren't even really each other's friends. Was there anyone else she could turn to? She liked her English teacher. She really did. But she didn't trust her by a long shot. She knew there were rules at school. Nothing was ever confidential. Adults always encouraged students to approach them, but that meant nothing to her. As far as she was concerned, the minute she opened her mouth would be the moment all hell would break loose. Jack would find out. She knew he would. And that terrified her. It terrified her to think about what he would do next. He had so much power over her. Not just over her. Everyone loved Jack. Those that loved him wanted to be like him and those that didn't knew they couldn't. She couldn't trust anyone. Not even herself at that point. She sat on the floor for hours and sobbed. Nobody would ever know what had happened that night and nobody would ever find out the truth. There was no way out. She knew this now and it absolutely terrified her.

She didn't remember falling asleep. She had found a few bits to eat in the kitchen. It seemed her mum had actually been shopping, even leaving Lauren a bit of lunch money.

Occasionally, her mum remembered that Lauren did need to eat.

Lauren had slept through. She had completely exhausted herself last night. And when she had finished, she had somehow made peace with the fact that this was her life now. It would all be over soon. One way or another, this nightmare would soon come to an end. And that's how Lauren had fallen asleep.

The next morning, Lauren woke up knowing that she had something to do. Something more than just the maths test and the English creative writing essay. That was one she had worked on over the past week, somehow. She had felt inspired by the question: 'What do you want others to know about you?'

She prepared for school, not forgetting her lunch money, her school bag and the pills her mum had left lying around. She took a deep breath, looked around and went upstairs to check on her mum. Her mum was lying there, staring at the ceiling. She didn't know what day of the week it was. She barely acknowledged Lauren's presence. It was OK. It was all OK. Lauren kissed her mum gently on the forehead, something she never did. 'I love you,' she whispered. She surprised herself. It was almost refreshing to let her guard down like this. As she left the room, she didn't notice her mum quietly whisper it back, tears in her eyes.

Lauren set off for school. For the first time in a long time, she heard the birds tweeting away; she felt the wind brush her face; she could see the light of day. Everything felt like it was happening for the very first time.

When she arrived at school, she was greeted by smirks and laughter. Her heart suddenly sank as her stomach churned. There they were everywhere, photographs of Lauren that night. The one from last night blown up and others she had never seen before. This couldn't be happening. It couldn't be. And as she reached her locker, there he was a few steps away, staring at her, an ice-cold look on his face. She could barely bring herself to open her locker, she was shaking so much. And there it was, the note, explaining what had taken place that night. *Had a great time. So easy spiking your drink. You didn't notice you were so busy pining over me. You're not the first and you certainly won't be the last. Carrying you upstairs was a doddle. That's the beauty of having so many mates. They'll do anything for you. Getting you into bed for a laugh was the highlight of the party. Don't flatter yourself though. I've had better. Oh, and messing you around since has just been the cherry on the cake. That's how I know you won't tell anyone. You're way too afraid. And even if you're not, who will believe you? Nobody really likes you. Nobody even notices you. Nobody would ever believe you over me. You know this; we both do. So do us all a favour and disappear. You'd be doing so many people a favour. Bye, Lauren, it's been fun. J.*

She knew what she had to do now. She knew it and she was OK with it. First though, she was going to hand in the paper. See Ms Williams one last time. You couldn't really call the essay her legacy, but she had put her heart and soul into that one. It was her paper, her way of getting noticed just once in her life, even if she wasn't there to see that moment. She walked to English, at peace with her decision. She held the paper in her hand, proud of her very last writing piece. She took a deep breath and walked in, trying really hard not to attract any attention to herself. Of course, this was never going to be the case. There was hissing, shouting, whistling and clapping. Was this really how everyone else spent their time? Did they really have nothing better to get on with? She supposed not. She looked down and took herself away from all the chaos. She shut her eyes and imagined herself far away from it all. As far as she could get. And just for a moment, she blocked out the noise and the chaos. She almost felt excited at the prospect of going on this journey more permanently. This would be her focus for the remainder of the class.

She didn't say a word. She didn't answer any questions the teacher asked. She didn't even attempt to look up at the class. She kept her head down, knowing that every passing minute was a minute closer to the end. And this was how she spent her time in English. When the bell rang, she walked up to Ms Williams. She handed in her paper, taking in this moment, her last. Her English teacher thanked her and spoke to her more warmly than anyone had in years. Lauren looked her straight in the eyes, taking in this unique moment of warmth and care. And then she took off.

She took the stairs straight to the girls' toilets and chose the largest cubicle there. Everything she needed was in her bag. She sat for a minute, reminiscing back to all those moments she had been met with in her life. The incessant arguments with her parents. The fights between her parents. The love she had watched other parents and their children share. The moment she stole her first book and taught herself to read. The moment she realised nobody would be there to congratulate her. The moment she got noticed at school for the first time. The night that would then go on to change her life. The misery she had lived since. And finally, Jack's cold calculating smile.

Science had never been her strong point, but even Lauren knew that three boxes of paracetamol were enough to finish you off, provided nobody found you in time. Hence why she waited for the bell to go, knowing this was likely to give her time to act. And she did, two tablets at a time. She placed Jack's note by the tablets, hoping that at the very least, somebody would notice it, hoping someone would read it and finally understand her pain.

35

By the time she reached the third box, she could feel herself getting weaker. She could feel her body slowly giving up and slipping away. She could feel herself beginning to fall asleep.

The last thing she remembered was the gentle kiss she placed on her mum's forehead. She would never know that her mum had felt her tender embrace and had looked back as Lauren walked away for the last time.

Lauren wouldn't live to see her seventeenth birthday. She would never know that she wasn't truly alone. Lauren would never get the chance to speak out. She would never find out whether or not Jack would be punished. As Lauren faded away softly, she finally felt the peace and happiness she had so desperately been searching for all her life.

By the time she was found, it was too late. Lauren had died. She had died alone and although she had never been noticed in life, she was certainly noticed now.

The Secret

Claudine woke up on the morning of her nineteenth birthday to find the first clue to her birthday surprise by her bedside. Every year, her parents made a fuss of her. They didn't see why this year had to be any different. Just because Claudine was a year into adulthood didn't mean she wasn't still their little girl. And Claudine had to admit she loved every minute of it!

Growing up, they had called themselves the three musketeers. They were like the three bears: Papa Bear, Mama Bear and Baby Bear. It was strange to everyone else but not to them. They were the perfect family.

Nineteen years in this world equalled nineteen clues to her birthday present. Today was going to be a long one! She'd become a pro at this game and was on her way to beating last year's record of twenty-nine minutes and thirty seconds.

She ran around the house like some overexcited child and didn't stop until her final clue.

'Go back to where you started and look for something blue. Once you know what we're talking about, it will find you.'

Her passport! That was it! Her parents had promised her a trip after her exams, after she'd spent months convincing them a gap year was the way to go for her. It had taken some persuading. If at first you don't succeed! And she did.

'Surpriiiiise! We wondered how long it would take you this year.' Her mother had been waiting in the kitchen. 'Your father's had to go out for a while. He's been called into work. He promised he would try and get away soon.'

'Twenty-eight minutes and fifty-nine seconds! That was a close shave!'

'Oh, well done, sweetheart. We know you're getting a little old for these games but we're still digesting the fact you turned eighteen last year.'

'I know, Mum.' Claudine didn't mind playing along. Just seeing the look on her mum's face each year was worth it.

'Listen, you get dressed, and we'll go out for breakfast, OK? Anything you want. My treat, of course.'

'Thanks, Mum. You really are the best!'

It took Claudine all of ten minutes to get ready. She knew this would be one of her last years at home with her mum and dad. The universities she'd applied for weren't in London, so she'd be moving out next year, like countless other students in the UK. None of her friends really understood why Claudine would rather be with her parents at the age of nineteen. They were all out clubbing or drinking. They just didn't get it. It wasn't the same for Claudine. To her, the most important people lived under the same roof. Nobody else really mattered. Her parents were devoted to her, and she was devoted to her parents.

'Where shall we go, darling? That lovely breakfast place you love so much?'

'No, Mum. That one's expensive. We don't need to go that far. And anyway, we're having dinner with Dad tonight, aren't we?'

'Yes, we are, Claudine. Of course we are. And your dad'll be back before dinner. He wouldn't miss that. But we thought that tonight, we could stay in. I know it's a little different from our usual celebrations, but we thought it would make a nice change.'

'Oh, right. Yes, of course, Mum. I don't mind what we do. As long as we're together as a family.'

'That's settled then, darling. I'll text your dad. Confirm. You can order anything you like!'

'Thank you, Mum, not just for this, but for everything you do for me. I know it's not always easy working such long hours. You and Dad have done so much for me. Don't think I don't appreciate it, because I do, Mum.'

Claudine's mum was her best friend. She could tell her mum anything, from school to boyfriends to anything she needed to talk about. They didn't keep secrets from each other. Her friends at school had always envied her in this way. It was like they didn't understand that her mum could be her best friend. They just didn't get it but then, they didn't have her mum.

'Order anything you want, darling. They've got some new smoothies on the menu. Shall we get one? No calorie counting today.'

'You're so sweet, Mum. Please stop worrying. I'm having a great time. With you, I always do. I promise.' Her mum sometimes needed reassurance on this. She was always worried she wasn't doing enough for her daughter, even though she went above and beyond every single time.'

'Thank you, sweetheart. Now tell me, any gossip? How's Amelia's love life?' Come to think of it, Claudine hadn't heard from Amelia as much since she'd got herself a boyfriend. This was Amelia all over. She was a great friend, but where men were involved, her judgement was non-existent.

'I haven't heard from Amelia lately to be honest, Mum. She can get like this sometimes, usually when there's a new man in her life. The last I heard of it, they were having the time of their lives. Whether or not this is true is a different story…'

'Should we be worried?' Claudine loved that her mum always used the pronoun *we*. As if her problems were her mum's problems. 'Now let's order.'

The food came under ten minutes later. Everything was mouth-watering. The pancakes, the smoothies and everything else they'd ordered was just delicious.

'Mum, this is all great. It really is. I couldn't have asked for a better birthday.'

'Oh, you're welcome, sweetheart. You deserve it all. Now hurry up and eat. We've got some shopping to do.'

They'd been in the café for about an hour. There was such a relaxed atmosphere. It was never too busy and the staff were just lovely. Everything on the menu was slightly overpriced but worth every penny.

Claudine's mum paid and they set off on their shopping trip. Oxford Street was their oyster!

'Remember, Claudine, you get to pick out three gifts. So, think carefully about what you want to choose.'

'Mum, I don't want you to go overboard. You've spent enough on me already. I know money's been tight lately. So, let's not get too carried away.'

'Claudine, that's not your problem. And anyway, your father and I are paying off our debts, so you have nothing to worry about. Now your father's back in employment, things should settle down.'

'Even so, Mum…'

'Right, that's enough out of you, young lady. Why don't we go to House of Fraser first. I've always loved it there.'

'You're the boss! Now lead the way.' Claudine knew she couldn't win this one. It was no use arguing about it.

Claudine and her mum spent their entire afternoon getting makeovers, picking out gifts and walking from store to store like the ladies of leisure they were destined to be. Claudine loved every minute of it and she could tell her mum did too.

It was past five when they had finished their shopping spree.

'Now that's what I call a day of shopping. Shall we get a taxi home, darling?'

'Mum, no! It'll cost a fortune to get back to Hammersmith. Let's get the tube today. Next time, we'll do things your way.' Before her mum could argue, Claudine dragged her to the tube station and they took the tube home.

'See, Mum? I told you it wouldn't take us long to get home this way!'

'I know, sweetheart. And you're right. My daughter, the wise one!'

'Shall I make us a cup of tea, Mum? Why don't you go and sit down. You must be exhausted.'

'That would be lovely, Claudine. A cup of tea is just what we need. Your father'll probably be leaving work soon. We've got a bit of time before he gets back.'

'Mum, thank you. For everything. You're just the best mum anyone could ever wish for.' Her mum looked like she was getting emotional. 'I'm sorry, Mum. I didn't mean to upset you.'

'No, no, you haven't. I'm just so grateful for these moments.'

'Are you sure that's all it is?' Claudine was wary. Her mum usually did a great job of insisting that she was fine, but this wasn't always the case.

Claudine had been worried about her mum, especially since her mum's illness. Growing up, Claudine had experienced her mum's depression for years, and although she'd been doing much

41

better for some time, Claudine was never quite convinced that her mum was telling her the truth.

'I'm fine, my love. I promise! Now you go and try on that new dress. It looks stunning on you. You can wear it tonight if you like. Oh, and don't forget the shoes!' Claudine knelt down and cuddled her mum for a few seconds. It was her way of checking on her mum when she couldn't get anything out of her.

'Right. I'd better get ready then! I'm looking forward to dinner with Dad.'

'Oh yes, me too, darling.' Claudine wasn't convinced her mum was OK but there was no point in insisting. She would check on her again later. For now, she had an outfit to fit into!

Claudine's dad got home about an hour later and they ordered dinner. Her mum insisted on bringing out the china plates and crystal glasses.

'You really don't need to do this, Mum. I know how much you value them. We can use the everyday plates you know.'

'Nonsense! It's your nineteenth birthday, sweetheart. It's only right.'

'She's right you know, Claudine. You're only nineteen once.' Claudine's dad was obviously getting into the party mood.

The food arrived and for once, it was on time. It really had been the perfect day.

'I'm so glad we've ordered Thai, sweetheart. That was a great idea.'

'Thanks, Dad. I'm glad you like it. You know how much I love Thai food.'

They had ordered so much and yet, by the end of the meal, there was nothing left. If there was one thing the three musketeers were good at, it was eating! They'd never participated in any food contests or anything, but they knew that if they ever did, they would win hands down!

'Let me clear up, Mum. Dad, you take Mum into the living room. I'll be in in a minute. We've had quite the day!'

'You're right, love. Come on, Irene.' He took her by the hand and led her into the living room. Claudine liked watching her dad being affectionate. He had become a true gentleman, especially since his wife's recovery.

Claudine joined her parents in the living room moments later, looking forward to the birthday cake she was about to taste. Her mum always baked the cake, every single year. It was all part of the birthday tradition.

'A toast to our darling daughter. One in a million.' Before she could say anything, her dad went on. 'Listen, sweetheart, there's something we've been wanting to talk to you about for a while now. We thought now was the right time to bring it up.'

'OK...' Claudine laughed. 'Should I be worried, Dad? Mum, are you OK?'

'Everything's fine, sweetheart. What I'm about to say doesn't need to change anything, so you have nothing to worry about.'

'OK, Dad. I am starting to worry now.'

'When you were just a baby, you were in need of a home.' Her dad was looking nervous. 'And we became the luckiest parents in the world when we brought you into ours.'

'But, Dad, I don't understand. What are you trying to say?'

'I'm trying to say, Claudine, that you're...'

'That you're adopted, sweetheart.' Her mum finished off the sentence, seeing how much her husband was struggling.

'Adopted? What are you talking about?' Surely this was some kind of practical joke. This was the first she had ever heard of it.

'Yes, adopted.' Her dad recomposed himself. 'We've wanted to tell you for so long, but the time was never right. You're nineteen now and…'

'And what? You thought you would give me one final birthday gift? One I wouldn't forget?' It was starting to dawn on Claudine that this was real.

'Look, sweetheart. We know it's a lot to take in. But like your father said, this doesn't have to change anything. We're still the same musketeers we were five minutes ago. We're still a family. And above all, we're still your parents and we love you so very much.'

'The same? Are you kidding me? You've just told me I'm adopted, and you expect me to believe that everything is still the same? Is this what today was all about, Mum? Butter me up before you throw me back down? I'm sorry. I can't do this. I need some space. I just can't believe it.' Claudine couldn't look her parents in the eye. She could barely even breathe. She needed to get away. She ran upstairs and slammed her bedroom door behind her.

'Leave her, Irene. She needs some space.' Claudine didn't hear a word after this. She didn't care to. Her parents had just dropped a hell of a bombshell on her and she had no idea what to do with it.

She sat on the edge of her bed, trying her very hardest to take in what she could only call a bombshell. Why now? Why wait this long to tell her? What the hell did they think was going to happen? That she was going to pat them on the back and tell them everything was going to be OK? They'd had years to mention it. 'Do you want milk on your cornflakes? Oh, by the way, Claudine, you're adopted.' Or maybe, 'Why don't we go for a walk? We need to talk about your adoption.' It really wasn't that difficult.

Claudine was just furious. On her birthday of all days. They'd made such a fuss every year. That was the one day where they all put their problems aside and came together to celebrate as a family. So why today? Why not tomorrow, or better still yesterday?

Claudine started pacing around her room. There really wasn't very far to go, but she couldn't help it. Emotion was getting the better of her. She wanted to open the window and scream. Yet what would that solve? She'd always been told not to air her laundry in public. Then again, she'd also been told she was her parents' daughter, so did that first statement really count?

How could they? Maybe she should just go and ask them. Better out than in, right? But what would they say? What was the point? *No, they can't get away with this!* Claudine stormed out of her room and prepared to face her parents. For the first time ever, she felt like they were no longer a team. She made sure to face them and look them both straight in the eye as she prepared to speak. They both looked so helpless, but she was too angry to care.

'Why? Why now? Why did you tell me this tonight? Did you think I'd jump into your arms and tell you how grateful I was to find this out? Did you think somehow this would bring us closer? I just can't get my head around this.'

Both her parents looked down. They were speechless.

'Look, Claudine…' Her mother evidently didn't know where to start.

'What? What is it, Mum? Are you going to feed me a sob story now? Tell me how you're the victim in all this? Do you know what? For years, I bought into it. When you were at your lowest, I made sure I could be there to pick you up. I was only twelve, Mum, but that didn't matter. All that mattered was that you were OK. And you know why? Because you were my mum. You always told me we didn't have any secrets. No matter how depressed you got, you always said we would be honest with each other.'

'Don't blame your mother, Claudine. She's been wanting to tell you for a while.'

'Oh, has she now? For how long? Nineteen years maybe? That's how long you've both had! NINETEEN YEARS and counting! And you, Dad, you sit there looking all upset, like you don't have a part to play in all this. For years, you were battling with your alcohol problems and for years, you were unemployed. I had to watch Mum pick up the mess you made time and time again. You were horrible to us for a while. You used to say all types of things and yet you never thought to include that I was adopted? Seriously, Dad?'

Claudine was breaking down. She could no longer keep it together. Was this why she put uni on hold? If she'd known this was the parting gift, she'd have left in the blink of an eye. She wouldn't even have considered sticking around, not for this.

'Oh, sweetheart... Come h...' Claudine didn't let her mum finish.

'No, don't bother. Don't come near me. I can't do this, not tonight. I can't sit here and play the doting daughter. Not now I know what I know. I need to get out of here.'

'Please don't, darling. Stay. We really need to talk about this.' Her mother was practically begging her to stay.

'Don't try and stop me. I don't want to stay here. I can't be around you right now. I just can't.'

She ran upstairs and picked up whatever she could find. She

knew it was late, but Amelia would still be up. She was a night owl and her evening was probably only just beginning. She called a cab. No point in wasting her so-called birthday money.

'Where are you going? Please, Claudine. Don't leave. Not now. You don't know just how much we love you. We know we should've told you sooner. You're absolutely right. But we were scared. We were terrified. We're so sorry, love.' Her mother was practically on the floor sobbing her heart out. Yet Claudine was too angry to look back. Up until tonight, she would've done anything to pick her mum up, but this was no longer her responsibility, not after what they'd just told her.

The cab arrived after just a few minutes. At that time of night, it was easy to get one, especially on a weekday. Weekends were a different story. As she got in, she didn't look back. She refused to be taken in by her parents any longer, if she could still call them that. Amelia had got back to her straight away. Of course, Claudine could stay with her. She didn't even need to ask.

As Claudine directed the cab driver to her friend's flat, she didn't stop to think about what she was feeling. There were no words right now. She just needed to get to Amelia's flat, and then she would figure out her next move. A good friend had once taught her to take one step at a time when she was feeling overwhelmed, and right now, she was definitely overwhelmed.

It took the driver all of half an hour to reach Amelia's flat in Wimbledon. She paid her fare and looked up to see her friend waiting at the bottom of the building. Claudine must've sounded really bad. It wasn't like Amelia to wait outside.

Amelia liked her comfort. She always had. She wasn't quite used to being disturbed. She paid a lot of money to live where she did and she liked it that way. Amelia had never been very good at saving up. She was a live in the moment kinda girl and it suited her just fine. But she always had time for her friends. She was loyal. This was something that Claudine had discovered the day her mum went into hospital. She'd reached rock-bottom and couldn't cope at the time. So, they had had no choice. Claudine remembered that day. She was only thirteen, yet Amelia, eighteen at the time, had come round and spent the night. Claudine would never forget that.

She walked over to Amelia who welcomed her in with open arms. Claudine knew she was in good hands.

'Happy birthday, lovely. It doesn't look like it's the birthday of your dreams, but here. I got this for you a while back.'

'Thanks, Amelia. You really shouldn't have, but thank you. Do you mind if I open it a little later? I promise I will.'

'Course. No rush. I'm guessing you'll be needing the spare room for a few days?'

'Is that OK?'

'Of course it is! Don't be stupid. You just make yourself at home. Let me just get a few bits ready. We don't need to talk tonight. I'll get the room ready for you, k? Be right back.'

'Thank you...' Claudine could feel herself getting emotional.

'Now, stop that! It's a bed. It needs company.' Amelia wasn't good at accepting compliments. They embarrassed her. She hated to be embarrassed, no matter who it was.

'You know what I mean!' Claudine smiled to herself.

Amelia prepared the room with the same love and care that she provided to all her guests. And about twenty minutes later, she reappeared.

'Now listen, as your friend, I'm going to tell you to go and get some sleep. You look shattered. Get some sleep and we'll talk in the morning, yeah? And listen, if you need anything, and I mean anything, come and get me.' Amelia had a maternal instinct in her, even though she hated to admit it.

'OK, thanks, Amelia. I could probably do with some sleep.' She didn't think she'd manage any sleep, but she didn't dare disobey Amelia. She was the boss!

Claudine picked up her things, realising she'd forgotten half of everything. She hadn't really thought this through… She knew Amelia would have everything to hand anyway, which she did. There was a toothbrush and a few toiletries by the side of her temporary bed and a spare pair of PJs. Amelia didn't do things by halves!

'You're the best, you know that?'

'I know, I know. That's what I'm renowned for. Now, go! See you in the morning.' Amelia winked at Claudine and walked back into the living room.

Claudine didn't know what to do with herself. As close as they were, she always felt an odd sensation if she wasn't in her own house, like somehow she wasn't safe. It was difficult to explain and not many people understood it but the feeling was there, at least for the first couple of nights. But then, she knew she wouldn't feel any safer at home anyway, so there was no point in worrying about it.

Claudine got ready for bed, as per her friend's orders, and turned her phone off. There were a ton of messages and missed calls but she wasn't in a good place and the last thing she wanted was to hear from anyone.

She hadn't recognised herself tonight. She wasn't used to being harsh. She wasn't a harsh person. She was usually the soft one, the one who was too busy solving everyone else's problems to worry about her own. But not this time. This time, she was bruised and the cut was deep.

Those were her last thoughts as she slowly drifted off. She didn't notice Amelia come in to check on her, nor did she hear her call her mother to let her know Claudine was safe. Claudine would probably kill her for doing it, but what she didn't know couldn't hurt her.

'Ready for some breakfast?' Amelia had laid out a feast, from toast to jam to pancakes to pastries.

'I know you've gone to a lot of trouble but I'm not hungry to be honest…'

'Not hungry? Woman, what's hunger got to do with this? I've laid out a proper five-star breakfast for you, better than the Ritz. You will eat it! Don't even think about making up an excuse. Don't forget who you're talking to!' Claudine knew Amelia meant business.

'OK… Fine, you win.' Even in her darkest moments, Amelia knew how to pick her up.

'That's more like it. Now sit! Earl Grey or English breakfast?'

'I don't know… You choose.'

'Earl Grey it is then.'

'No, no. I'll stick to English breakfast, thanks.'

'Oh, so there is still some life in there? Interesting!'

'OK, OK, I get your point. Thanks. I mean that.'

'Now, enough with the thank you. Eat! You're getting thinner by the minute.'

'No, I'm not!'

'No, you're not. But eat anyway.'

Amelia brewed a pot of tea and sat with Claudine.

'You have my undivided attention. What's going on, lovely?' Amelia wasn't one to beat about the bush.

'I don't know where to start. Yesterday, everything was so... perfect, so normal. And then they had to go and tell me that.' Claudine put the pastry down. She couldn't stomach it right now.

'Don't think you're getting away with not eating, young lady. I've got my eye on you.' Amelia grinned at Claudine, trying to lighten the mood a little. It wasn't easy. 'Anyway, what do you mean? Tell you what?'

'You're not gonna believe this, Amelia.'

'Come on, girl. Spit it out. Don't do this to yourself. The longer you keep it in, the harder it'll be to tell me.'

'God, you can be direct sometimes.'

'Didn't you know? I'm renowned for my diplomacy skills. Now come on, seriously, talk to me.'

'I'm adopted, Amelia.' Claudine could feel a shiver down her spine as she uttered the words out loud for the first time.

'What? Adopted? What the hell?'

'I know, right? I know there's no such thing as the perfect family, but this...'

'Bloody hell, Clauds. I don't know what to say!'

'You? Speechless? Pull the other one.'

'I'm sorry, lovely. I really am. I know it must be a shock. That's why you need more food. Get that pastry down you. The pancakes are next.' Amelia could never be serious for too long.

Showing too much emotion made Amelia uncomfortable. This was both an advantage and a challenge for Claudine. She'd always worn her heart on her sleeve. She was always conscious of getting too emotional in front of Amelia, who just wasn't that sort of friend. But Claudine knew that Amelia was a good egg. She was there when Claudine needed her and that was what mattered.

'I don't know what I'm going to do. I can't get my head

around this. One minute, we're playing happy families and the next, we're breaking up. All in the space of an hour.'

'Look, you can't think that way. They love you. That's obvious. They'd do anything for you. And that's more than can be said for most parents.'

Growing up, Amelia didn't have her mum around. She was six when her mum had decided to run away with her latest beau, leaving her to fend for herself and her dad. He had tried his very best to be a good dad to Amelia, but he often got it wrong. She never went without. Her dad at least made sure of that. But Amelia had spent her entire childhood giving her dad the benefit of the doubt. She couldn't risk him running out on her as well, so she made the best of her situation.

'I know. I'm sorry. I didn't mean anything by that, Amelia.'

'Don't be silly. I'm not asking you to feel sorry for me or anything. I just don't want you to do anything stupid, like throw away the family you've got.'

'You're only saying that because you've always really liked them.'

'And so what if I do? They're good people, Clauds. They've given you a roof over your head. They've fed you. They've made you the person you are today. I wouldn't be friends with you otherwise. Look, all I'm saying is, don't be too hard on them. At least give them a chance to explain. I'm going out in a bit. Why don't you call your mum and see if she can come round for a bit?'

'Oh no, look. I'm not ready to see them yet. I know you're right and I will think about it. But I need a bit of time to myself.'

'OK, fine. I get it. You know I do. But don't leave this too long. You need them and they need you, even if you don't realise it yet.'

Amelia got ready to go and left Claudine with her thoughts.

This was dangerous for Claudine. When she let her thoughts wander off, she drove herself crazy. But it seemed that Amelia had made sure this didn't happen.

'Hello, darling...' Amelia had let Claudine's mum in before leaving the flat to them.

'I could kill her! Mum, what are you doing here? How did you know I was here?' Claudine knew the answer to her question. It was all Amelia's handiwork.

'Don't be angry at Amelia. She's only trying to help.' Her mum knew she was on shaky ground.

'What are you doing here, Mum? I told you last night. I'm not ready to see you or Dad. Is he with you?'

'No, Claudine. It's just me today.' Irene was letting her daughter lead the conversation.

'Right. Let me guess. You've come hoping to take me home, pick up where we left off?'

'No, of course not, darling. I've come because...' Claudine quickly cut her mum off.

'Don't *darling* me as if we can just magically get back to the way things were.'

'You're right, I'm sorry. I've come because, well, I thought you might have some questions. I thought you might want to talk. I know how confusing all this must be.'

'Do you? Do you really? Last night, I thought I belonged to this family. I thought that it was just you, me and Dad. And then you go and tell me that everything I've believed my whole life is based on a lie.'

'Don't say that, Claudine. Of course it's not.'

'Isn't it? For goodness' sake, Mum, we're not even related. You're not even my mum!'

'Now, young lady, don't you ever say this to me again!

Don't even think it. I am your mum. That's non-negotiable!' The cards had turned slightly here.

'I'm just so confused, so lost I guess.' Claudine was letting her guard down very slightly. 'My whole life, I've thought we were a family, and now, I just don't know what to believe. I have so many questions I can't answer. I've been trying to answer them all night. It's just not happening. I've woken up feeling more lost than I was last night.'

'OK, then, sweetheart. Ask away. Ask me anything you want and I'll try my best to answer. First, can I have a cup of tea? Let's do this the good old-fashioned way. Let me make us one.' Irene was trying to take a more relaxed approach if that was even possible after last night. It seemed to be working. Nobody could make a cup of tea like her mum could, and nobody could drink it like Claudine.

'I don't know where to start…'

'Just ask whatever's on your mind. Don't worry about upsetting anyone.' Irene knew this conversation had been a long time coming.

'Erm, OK… How old was I when you adopted me?'

'You were just a little baby. You were two months old, the most beautiful thing we'd ever seen. We fell in love with you there and then.'

'Why did you adopt me?' The questions were coming to Claudine now. It was going to be an emotional morning.

'You were just perfect. You were such a happy little baby. The first time we met you, we knew you were our daughter.'

'No, that's not what I meant.' Claudine was still feeling bitter. 'Why did you choose to adopt?'

'Oh…' This was not an easy one to answer.

'Be honest with me, Mum. No secrets and no lies.' Claudine

54

was still calling her mum. That was something. Irene knew she had to do right by her daughter if she didn't want to lose her altogether.

'OK, well, your father and I were told a year before that we couldn't have children. God knows we tried to conceive. We put our heart and soul into making a baby. But when we'd been trying for two years and I wasn't getting pregnant, we bit the bullet and contacted the doctor. He sent us for tests. We found out your father couldn't have children. He was devastated.'

'Is that when he started drinking?'

'Yes, it was. And no matter how many times I told him it didn't matter, he didn't believe me. It's almost like he felt he wasn't good enough anymore, like somehow this made him less of a man. But I came to terms with it. I had to. I loved your father and I knew that there was a way. So, when the doctor suggested adoption, I jumped at the idea. Your father needed a little persuading, but he eventually came round to the idea as well.' Claudine knew her mum was being honest. It wasn't an easy conversation for her either.

'Why have you waited this long to tell me?'

'That's a valid question. I guess we were scared, terrified even. We knew when you found out, there was a chance you would stop seeing us as your parents. And that was the last thing we wanted.'

'So, the depression…'

'Partly, yes. I've always tried to be the best mum I could for you. But I never felt like it was enough. I never felt like I was doing enough.'

'But, Mum, you were. Of course you were.'

'I certainly tried. But I don't know…'

'And my birth…' Claudine couldn't bring herself to say it.

55

Feelings of guilt were creeping in.

'It's OK, darling. You can say it.' Irene was trying hard not to let her daughter see how tough this was. She didn't have the right to, not now.

'My birth parents. Who are they?' Claudine couldn't believe she had to ask the only mum she'd known about her birth parents.

'We only ever met your birth mother. She was very young when she had you, barely eighteen at the time.' Claudine's mum had been younger than Claudine was now.

'Do you remember what she was like?' Claudine could see her mum was suffering. This was no doubt tough on her, but Claudine had to know.

'She was petite and pretty like you. She had big green eyes and her smile, well, let's just say she passed it down to our precious little girl.'

'Oh, Mum, don't cry. I didn't mean to upset you.' Claudine felt terrible. She knew the toll this conversation was having on her mum.

'You didn't. It's OK. I promise.' Irene tried her very best to reassure her daughter, even if she didn't know if everything would be OK. 'We only ever met her a few times. The last time we saw her was the day she gave you up. Her name was Emily.'

'Emily? Oh...' Claudine wondered what she should ask next. She was worried about what her mum would say to her next question.

'Why did she give me away, Mum? Didn't she want me?'

'You have to understand, Claudine, your mum was very young, and she wasn't very well. She was younger than you are now. She was still a child when she got pregnant.'

'I know that, but...'

'Don't hate your mum, Claudine. If it wasn't for her, I

wouldn't be standing in front of my beautiful, precious little girl right now.'

'Do you… have an address for her?'

'Your father never wanted me to keep it. You have to understand, he loved you so much. We both did. He was terrified of losing you. You know men deal with things differently to women. He didn't know what was for the best. Neither of us did.'

'Do you still have that address?' Claudine was focused on her questions. She needed answers and it was now or never.

'I thought you might want it. Here.' She took a piece of paper out of her bag and reluctantly handed it to her daughter. 'Listen, sweetheart. If you have to find your birth mother, I'll understand and I'll make your father understand it too, but just be careful, OK? And remember, no matter what, we're your parents.'

'Thanks for the address, Mum.'

'Listen, sweetheart. I mean it. We're your parents. That's not going to change overnight. I'll understand if you need to find her, but know that I'll be waiting. We both will.'

Irene rushed over and squeezed her daughter for a few seconds. She knew their conversation had come to an end. It was her cue to leave. Before she walked out, she uttered a few final words to her daughter.

'I mean it, sweetheart. We love you. And when you're ready, we'll be waiting. So come home anytime you want. Just don't wait too long. We miss you.'

Irene left and waited till she was a few seconds away before bursting into tears. She didn't know that back at Amelia's flat, her daughter was doing the same.

Claudine was feeling very confused. She didn't know whether to be eternally grateful to her best friend, or whether she hated her guts for calling her mum. She didn't know what to make of the conversation she'd just had with her mum either. She knew how difficult it must have been for her mum to open up in this way. But then, her mum had always worn her heart on her sleeve, just like her. Like mother like daughter. Claudine knew this conversation couldn't change anything between them, not right now anyway. But at least she'd got some answers. Were they the answers she was hoping for? What was she even hoping for? She had no idea what she was feeling right now.

She tried keeping herself busy. She hadn't cleared up the royal breakfast Amelia had set out for them yet. Amelia would be back soon, so that was the plan until she did. She felt like the address she didn't dare look at was staring straight at her, somehow just waiting for Claudine to respond. But the moment she did, she knew what it meant. It meant that she would have to decide whether to act on it, or just bury it along with the secret her parents had forced on her.

When Amelia did at long last make it back, Claudine was in full cleaning mode.

'OK, don't kill me! I knew you would never let me ring your mum if you knew. But she's your mum and she needed to know. I love you but I can't have you moving in! That was a joke by the way. How did it go?'

'I should hate you right now. You know that?'

'But you don't. How can you? This lovable face? It's the one Marcus is falling for as we speak!'

'I don't hate you. I love you for caring. I just…'

'You just don't know what the hell to do with everything you know.'

'Exactly. And my mum's given me the address.'

'What address? Oh, you mean… *that* address?'

'Yeah – my birth mum's address.'

'Wow! That must've killed her.'

'I know and I shouldn't but I just feel so guilty. She told me to ask her anything so I did. But I know she was dying inside.'

'Of course, she was, hun. She brought you up. She's your mum! But I get it. You need to know.'

'What do I do now?'

'Now? Now, we get googling.'

'What? You mean I should…?'

'Yes, of course, you should meet her. Look, if you do, you might like her or you might hate her. But one way or another, you'll be able to move forward. If you don't, you'll spend the rest of your life just wondering. Who is she? Does she look anything like me? Why did she give me away?'

'I guess…'

'You know I'm right. Tell me, where does this wonder woman live?'

'I don't know…'

'What do you mean you don't know? The address is right there, screaming at you!'

'I can't do it… Can you look for me?'

'Another favour? You owe me, woman!'

'Yeah, yeah, now just look and tell me.'

'OK, she lives in Lewisham.'

'Lewisham? Right.'

'Like I said, let's get googling. I'll drive.'

Claudine took a breath. This was all happening too fast. She couldn't handle it. Just a few days ago, she thought she had it all figured out. She thought she had a loving family behind her. And now, she was getting ready to go and meet a woman who was apparently her mother? This couldn't be happening.

'Amelia, I don't think I can do this. Not right now. I think I'm gonna be sick.'

Before she knew it, she was in the bathroom bringing her breakfast back up. Now was definitely not the time to meet this woman, not while she was feeling like this. First impressions and all that.

'Clauds, are you OK?' She could hear Amelia shouting from a distance.

'Not really... I think I need to go back to bed to be honest.' Thank God for that. It was never ideal to feel this way, but ironically, it couldn't have come at a better time.

'All right, hun. You do that. Leave the rest to me.' Was Claudine hearing her right? What did she mean by this? She couldn't deal with that right now. She could barely drag herself to bed as it was. Everything else could wait.

The last thing she remembered was leaving the bathroom. She certainly didn't remember getting into bed.

'You fainted, hun. Talk about getting attention!' Amelia was sat at her bedside. 'I'm worried about you. I'm supposed to meet Marcus in an hour but I can cancel. Anything for you.' Amelia tried to laugh this one off, but she seemed genuinely worried about her friend.

'No, don't do that. You go. I'll be fine. I'm due a date with sleep anyway. I guess I just couldn't handle it. Sorry.'

'Don't be stupid. I pushed you too hard. Your mum turning up was a big enough shock for today. I shouldn't have insisted. I'm sorry, Clauds.'

'You? Sorry? Pfff. Now who's being stupid? You've been amazing. I've gotta admit, even calling my mum was a good surprise in a weird kinda way. Don't tell her though, yeah? I'm not ready for that yet.'

'Your secret's safe. But listen. If you need anything, and I mean anything, just call. Promise?'

'Promise. Now go! Don't keep him waiting. You know what men are like.'

Amelia got up and left the room reluctantly. Her love life could wait. Her friend needed her.

'I said go.'

'OK, OK! I'll be back soon, I swear.'

In a strange sort of way, it was a relief for Claudine to be left alone for a while. Her head was pounding and as much as she loved Amelia, it felt good to have some space. It was time to get some sleep and forget the reality she was living in for a while.

Claudine shut her eyes and pictured her younger self. She drifted off to sleep, feeling safe again in her past, a past that she was trying her hardest to hold onto.

Claudine was losing count of the days. She was lost in a world she didn't recognise. It took her about a week to start feeling healthy again. This whole situation had taken its toll and she had anticipated every moment. She was starting to feel better which meant that Amelia would soon be pushing her to meet the woman who was supposedly her mother.

'You're getting your colour back. You had me worried for a while. Listen, I know you've been putting our little conversation off, but you can't put it off forever.'

'I know. And I know you think I should meet this woman. And I know you've got the car out the front, ready to drive me at any given moment. But I'm scared, OK? I don't know what I'm going to find when I get there. This woman obviously didn't want me. Do I really want to hear her say those words to me?'

'You know it's not about that. My mum didn't want me and

I never got the chance to confront her. She never gave me the opportunity. But you do. You have a chance here to say your piece. Are you really going to let that go to waste? Aren't you just a little bit curious?'

'No, I'm not! Well, I mean, maybe a little. But is that enough? My whole world's been torn apart in the last week, Amelia.'

'I know it has, hun. But remember we said we weren't going to wallow in self-pity this week? There's plenty of time for that. You've got the rest of your life to feel sorry for yourself.'

'OK, look, fine. You're right. We'll do it. We'll go. Just give me a bit of time.'

'I've done that, hun. I've given you time. Now, we do things my way.'

'What? But I'm not ready yet.'

'Yes, you are. Don't give me that. You don't think I know you've been feeling better since yesterday? You don't think I know you're avoiding me because you know what you need to do?'

'But I…'

'Exactly, now stop talking to me and start getting ready.'

'Ready…?'

'Seriously, that's enough! Get ready and I'll see you in fifteen minutes. No more arguments.'

Claudine never was very good at arguing her case, especially not where Amelia was concerned. Amelia was too persuasive and she never gave Claudine enough time to defend herself. Amelia always ended up winning the battle.

'You can't bottle on me now! Make yourself beautiful and we can show this Emily what she's been missing out on for the last nineteen years!'

'If you say so…'

'Stop that right this instant! You are a gorgeous, intelligent young woman and you have nothing to feel insecure about. Right, are you ready? I certainly am.'

'Not yet… I still have to put some make-up on.'

'Leave that for the journey. You'll have ages.'

They set off arm in arm. Amelia knew she was challenging her best friend but if she didn't, who would? If she left this to Claudine, she'd probably still be in bed next year!

Amelia drove and talked the whole way through. She was a confident driver. Come to think of it, she was generally confident at anything she set her mind to. Claudine really admired that about Amelia. She could never figure out how Amelia did it, but hopefully she would teach her one of these days.

'I'm nervous. I don't know what I'll say. Where do I start?'

'That's an easy one. How about asking her why she abandoned you and what the hell she was thinking?'

'I don't know if I can manage that…'

'Well, if you can't, I certainly can!'

It was funny how the one time Claudine didn't mind the traffic, there was no traffic. Ironic, wasn't it.

'Right, we're here. It's that house I think.' Amelia was a confident driver indeed. And for some unknown reason, she knew London like the back of her hand.

'What? Are you sure?'

'Yes, now get out of the car and follow me!'

They both got out and Claudine made sure to put her arm around Amelia. It was her way of telling Amelia not to let her do this on her own.

It was a quiet street full of bungalows. It seemed that this woman had been living life in all its simplicity. Claudine didn't know what to make of any of this. When they got to the door, Amelia was the one to knock. If she left it to Claudine, they would still be there a week from now.

'Nobody's answering. Let's just go. We can say we tried.' Claudine sighed with relief at the prospect that this woman would never answer.

'No! I haven't come all this way for nothing. She owes me answers too.'

'How do you figure that one?' Claudine had a feeling Amelia was battling her own issues.

'How dare she leave my best friend! Just abandon her like some orphan. Who does this woman think she is?' Amelia meant business here and Claudine knew she wasn't talking about Emily.

'You won't find anyone in there.' A voice suddenly appeared out of thin air. They turned around to find an older lady talking to them. She must've been in her late seventies. 'Poor old Emily was taken ill recently. Mind you, she'd been ill for a long time. That's what drugs can do to you.'

'Oh… And do you know when she'll be back? We were hoping to speak to her.' Claudine was slowly gaining the confidence she needed, probably because she wasn't speaking to Emily herself.

'She won't be back. The poor girl died last week.' The lady looked to the floor. She seemingly felt very sorry for this woman. 'Anyway, who are you? Can I be of any assistance? I live just next door.'

'Oh no, no. Thank you. We were looking to speak to Emily. It's all right. Thanks anyway.' Claudine didn't know whether to feel relieved or upset at the news of this woman's passing. The lady smiled at both Claudine and Amelia and walked away.

'Wow! I wasn't expecting that one.' Amelia never had been

very good at hiding her surprise. Claudine on the other hand didn't say a word. 'Come on. Let's get out of here. I need a drink!'

The drive back should've felt much shorter, but it really didn't. Claudine and Amelia didn't say a word to each other. Amelia kept her eye on the road and Claudine closed hers, managing to shut off the world for the duration of the journey home.

They eventually got back and Claudine headed to her room. She needed to be alone. Amelia knew better than to argue. Tomorrow was another day and they would speak about today's events then. For now, they both just needed to rest, away from the world and away from each other.

Claudine came out of her room the next morning to find Amelia sitting at the kitchen table.

'Your dad's been in touch, Clauds. Your mum isn't doing too well. He didn't want to say anything until now. He thought she could handle the situation but she's getting worse. She's going back into depression, Clauds.'

Claudine didn't know what Amelia expected her to say. She decided against saying anything. She could see this was frustrating to her best friend.

'Clauds, are you serious? You're seriously just gonna stand there like some ungrateful little girl and ignore the fact that your mum's ill again? Seriously?'

'Oh whatever, Amelia.'

'Whatever? Are you serious? No, not whatever! You don't get to play that card. I get it, your mum and dad lied to you. They should've told you the truth years ago. I won't argue with you there. But are you seriously going to stand there, indifferent to what I'm saying? Well, I'll tell you something. I won't stand for it! You are not a little girl anymore. It's time you grew up. That's a lesson I was taught a long time ago.'

'Yes, we all know the story. Your mum left you. Your dad wasn't much of a dad. But look at you. You've got everything you need now. He bought you this flat and made sure you were comfortable.'

'Everything I need? Seriously? You think because I don't talk about it, it doesn't hurt? A few days ago, you discovered you had not one but two mums. And when you found that out, you chose to walk away from the parents that have done everything for you for the last nineteen years. And what did they do? They practically begged you to come home. Yet you responded by walking away. You walked away even though you knew what this would do to them. You know your mum's history, Claudine!'

'My mum?'

'Yes, your mum! The woman who's been there for you for the last nineteen bloody years. The woman who's been there, who's educated you, fed you, made sure you had a roof over your head. The woman who has loved you. Do you know that she's been on the phone to me every night since you left crying her eyes out because she thinks she's lost her precious little girl? Well, I'll tell you something. Her precious little girl is being a precious little brat right now. I love you, Clauds, but I love your parents too. And I'm not going to stand here and let you act like this while they're suffering the way they are. So, you shout all you want, ignore me even, but at the end of all that, you consider what's important. I'm going out!' Amelia slammed the door behind her, too furious to look back.

'Fine!' Claudine stood in the hallway. She was starting to feel stupid. She hated to admit it, but Amelia was right. It was time for her to take a long hard look at herself and think about everyone else.

For the first time in a while, Claudine decided it was time to face the music. Amelia usually disappeared for a good few hours when she was in this mood. This would give Claudine the time she needed to think about her next move. What was she doing here? Amelia was right. Her mum needed her. She pictured her lying in bed, unresponsive, alone in her thoughts. She pictured her dad, trying his best to get through to her mum but not having any luck. The only person her mum had ever wanted to get better for was Claudine.

Who was Emily? Some woman she'd never even met she apparently shared DNA with. Was it really fair to let the last nineteen years go for a woman who would never be in her life? God, she hated it when Amelia was right!

Claudine waited for Amelia to come home. It took a good few hours, but Claudine didn't have the right to say anything at this point, especially after everything her best friend had done for her.

'Don't mind me. I'm not staying.' Amelia was still angry. This wasn't going to be an easy conversation.

'I'm sorry. I'm really sorry. You were right. I was being an idiot this morning. What is it you called me? A spoiled little brat?' Claudine couldn't help but laugh.

'It was precious little brat. Don't start all right?'

'Oh, come on. Listen, I'm really sorry, OK? The last few weeks have been tough for me. And I don't know how it happened, but I've become a person I don't even really recognise.'

'I have to agree with you on that one.' Amelia was starting to let her guard down.

'It's just one minute I have parents, then I don't, though I know that technically I still do. Then I discover there's this other person I've never met before, and before I even go to meet her, I find out she's dead. I don't know how to deal with that, Amelia.' Claudine was being completely honest, both with Amelia and with herself. 'I know how much my mum loves me, and I guess that her depression is starting to make more sense to me now than it did before.'

'That's why you've got to go home, Clauds. You can't just keep avoiding it.' Amelia knew what Claudine had to do. 'I'm not kicking you out or anything, but Marcus is moving in tonight.'

'Oh, shut up. I get it. You're right. I do need to go home. I'm not gonna pretend I'm over it all, because I'm not. I'm still angry. I'm still… I don't even know what I am.'

'And you won't until you face this. Why don't you stay one more night and I can read you a bedtime story?'

'Whatever. No seriously, it's OK. I need to get home, don't I? I need to face the music, and I need to make sure my house and the people in it are still in one piece.'

Claudine's bags were ready. They were waiting for her by the door.

'Wow! You don't waste any time, do you? I'll let Marcus know. He'll be thrilled.'

'Right, yeah. I'll have to come and meet him one of these days.'

'You will!'

'And listen, I'm really sorry about how selfish I've been. This whole thing must've brought up a lot for you too. I'm here you know. I don't say it much but I am.'

'Don't get all mushy on me! Just get down there and get in

the car.'

'Right, yes.'

The drive was longer this time. The traffic was back. Life went on apparently.

'What will I say when I get home?' Claudine was starting to feel nervous again.

'Actions speak louder than words, lovely. Just go in and show your face. Take it from there.'

After about three quarters of an hour, they made it to Claudine's house.

'I'll call you!' Amelia knew that if she didn't rush Claudine a little, they'd be stuck in the car for the rest of the day.

'You do that. And listen, thanks for... well, everything.' Claudine was getting emotional.

'Yes, I know. Now go in! I'm leaving.'

By the time Claudine turned around to wave goodbye, Amelia had driven off. She stared at her house as if she was seeing it for the first time. She took a breath and walked to the door. For a moment, her thoughts took her back to her childhood and all the times her mum had been there to comfort her after a difficult day at school. She thought about all the times her mum had nursed her, helped her with her homework and looked after her when she couldn't look after herself. She remembered the countless times her dad had taken her to the park and bought her treats. She realised just how safe she had felt with her parents growing up and just how lucky she was to have them both. Claudine was seeing everything clearly for the first time in a long time. A weight had been lifted and she was finally home. Today was the first day of the rest of her life.

In the Name of Honour

Alissia woke up and for a moment, she wondered where she was. It took her a few seconds to realise that she was getting married tomorrow. Tomorrow was the big day. At least it was meant to be. All around her were people congratulating her on this life achievement. Everyone was so excited. Her family, her friends, her acquaintances. It was almost like they were the ones getting married. It was what you called *a family affair*.

Alissia lay in bed for what felt like hours, thoughts and questions racing through her mind. She let herself be drawn into her thoughts, dark as they were. This would be the only time she would be alone and given space. An hour from now, the preparations would begin and Alissia would be pulled around left, right and centre.

Alissia didn't dare think about how much had been spent on this wedding. She was the eldest, the first born. Her parents had been saving up since the day she was born, or at least, that's what she was made to believe. They had probably been saving long before she was born. They were giving her their dream wedding. And in exchange for this very expensive affair, she was letting them.

She had been told countless times about how lucky she was. But then, what did they know? What did all these people around her really know? Opinions flew out of their mouths all day long. Being the dutiful daughter that she was, she let them get away with their comments, countless comments day in, day out. Half the time, she wanted to tell them just how stupid they sounded and the other half, she wanted to shrivel into a tiny little ball and hide as far away as she possibly could.

Alissia had met her future husband on a number of occasions, at family gatherings, family dinners, family get-togethers. Funny how every time she did meet him, family was involved. What was it they were afraid of? That she would get to know him a little too well, or that she would get to know him at all.

Alissia was the eldest of three. She was 'blessed' with a younger sister and a most obliging brother. Growing up, she had been asked constantly to set the example. And she had tried. At least she thought she had. Except, nothing she ever did really felt good enough. The siblings each had their roles. Her little sister was the baby of the family, getting away with everything in God's name, and her brother was the honour of the family. He was the future man of the Matoushi household, the future king one might say. Sometimes, it felt like he was as bad as her father, just as strict and just as good a spy.

Alissia remembered her first day at university three years ago. She had overheard her father and brother speaking.

'Keep an eye on your sister today. Make sure she doesn't get too comfortable leaving the house. I trust you, son.'

'Of course, Father. You have my word.'

His *word*. Actually not just his word, his word of *honour*, because that was what it was all about. *Honour*. Alissia knew this. She wondered in fact, if it hadn't been her first word. It had most probably been her brother's.

How petrifying that first day at uni had been. She had made her way to City University with time to spare, hoping to look around beforehand. She knew her brother would soon be lurking around like some stalker. Her father had asked him to pick her up. She hadn't argued. She knew the score.

When she first set foot in the campus, she was blown away by the quantity of students walking around, probably just as amazed and overwhelmed as she was. She wasn't sure who to speak to. All around her were students laughing, chatting, acting like the eighteen year-olds they were. *I bet their parents actually hope their child will enjoy their first day in the real world!* Hers certainly didn't.

She had been waiting for her first lecture for what felt like ages. She didn't mind though. She longed to find her place in the world she was about to enter: the world of philosophy.

'I'm Lola. This is Peter.' Alissia turned around to be greeted by two smiling faces.

'Oh, hi! I'm Alissia…' Her throat was beginning to close in. She hadn't had a conversation with anyone in months. After school had ended, her parents had decided to keep her at home, worried that anyone from the outside world would corrupt her mind somehow. Even the day of her results, they had asked for her final grades to be posted. She had begged them not to. She had begged to see her friends one more time before they all left for their universities, but no. This was a battle she hadn't won. She was too argumentative, too rude and not dedicated enough to the family. 'Enough!' had yelled her father. When he yelled, you didn't talk back. You got the message. And the message only needed to be uttered once.

'Are you OK? You look a little stressed. It's all stressful, isn't it? First day! I feel like a child again.'

'Tell me about it.' Peter joined in, finally able to cut off Lola. 'I haven't slept for a week. Our future awaits us…'

'Oh… So, you're taking this course too?' Alissia smiled, so

grateful that someone had come to speak to her.

They made their way into the lecture hall. Alissia could tell Lola was a do-gooder. Front row seats it was. Alissia didn't dare contradict her, afraid that she'd be abandoned before she even got started.

'After you.' Peter winked just as Alissia walked past. She could feel her face heating up.

The lecture went on for two hours and Alissia loved every moment of it. 'The questions, the thoughts and the philosophers who inspired them'. What more could a girl want? And then the teacher ended the lesson and she remembered she was going home. Her brother would without a doubt be waiting at the gates, just like parents do when they're waiting for their five year-old.

'Do you fancy going for a drink, Alissia? Peter and I thought we'd explore the campus a little. We're staying just around the corner. That's how we met. Are you staying close by? I've never been away from home. This is the first time. My mum and dad were glad to see the back of me! Anyway, are you free?'

Peter gazed up at Alissia and looked into her eyes. It lasted only for a second, but what a second it was. Alissia felt herself heating up again.

'I'm sorry… I have to go… But maybe some other time.'

'Oh, come on. It'll be great! There's a load of societies you can join. I've already found about seven I can't wait to put my name down for. Peter, you've found a few as well, right? Hang on, let me find the leaflets.'

'Don't leave me alone with her… Please!' Alissia giggled to herself like a schoolgirl.

'I'm sorry… I really have to go now.'

'Oh, well, OK. Oh! Let me give you my number! Give me your phone. Peter, you put your number in too.' Alissia searched her bag for the phone and handed it to them. This wasn't a good idea… Hopefully, she'd have time to change the names. She'd done it before, she could do it again.

'Thanks—I'd better run.'

'At least let us walk you out! Come on!' Alissia knew this wasn't a good idea. But Lola wasn't taking no for an answer and Peter was silently begging her to stick around.

'OK, well, this is me. Thanks so much, guys. I'd better run but thank you.' The panic in Alissia's voice was getting stronger. She could feel it. She knew her brother was around somewhere and this terrified her.

'It was really great to meet you, Alissia. Stay in touch, won't you?' It was Peter speaking this time, looking her straight in the eyes. Alissia could have melted if there'd been any time.

She practically ran away without saying goodbye, hoping to make it look like she was the one waiting. But she looked up and there he was, waiting just as she'd thought.

'Who were they? And who's that boy? Dad's not going to like this!'

'They're nobody. They're just students. They were asking for directions.' Alissia couldn't think of anything else to say to her brother.

'It didn't look like that to me. Don't bullshit me, Alissia. Anyway, Dad'll want to know. Let's go. You're late as it is.'

That night had been hell. There was no other word. Her father had been waiting for a full report and that's exactly what he got. Thankfully, Alissia had just managed to hide the numbers before having to explain herself yet again and before he could look through her phone. She'd turned the notifications off too so he wouldn't know if someone texted. But then, she hadn't sent them her number yet so she was safe for now.

She'd had to miss the rest of the first week as the mark on her face had stayed visible longer than anticipated. Alissia had practically locked herself in her bedroom that week, more determined than ever to study, hoping that one day, just one day, the studying would pay off.

Alissia looked at the clock. Seven-thirty a.m. She knew that in just under half an hour, her day would begin. She dreaded to think about it. Women and girls everywhere. Her mother would be running around like a headless chicken, while her father sucked up to the family of the husband-to-be, honouring them every way he could think of. Her brother would be following her father around. He had probably been given orders which he couldn't wait to follow, eager to please his father at every chance. As for her younger sister, well, she would enjoy the chaos, the loud noise and the attention. Once Alissia was married off, her younger sister would have the privilege of being in her shoes.

Oh, how different they were. Alissia loved the simple pleasures of life. Often, while Alissia was engrossed in her latest novel, usually a nineteenth century classic, her sister would be shopping online to see what expensive gifts she could find for herself. Her parents never said no to her. She was the youngest and revelled in the attention she received. Alissia however was the eldest. She didn't have quite the same luxury, but then in all honesty, she had never wanted it. What she had wanted was much greater. It was something money couldn't buy. It was happiness.

Happiness didn't exist in this culture as one knew it. It was about family and honour, not individual happiness. At least, this was her understanding. At school growing up, she had heard friends talking constantly about happiness, and about how they wanted to be happy, how their parents were happy for them. Yet this was a concept that was foreign to cultures like hers and so she never bothered to share her own feelings about this. It did explain why today of all days, she was feeling far from *happy*.

Alissia couldn't bring herself to get up. She couldn't bring herself to do anything. All she wanted was to forget what was happening. Or maybe all she wanted was to be a lot more like her sister. Her sister didn't mind all this. This life was exactly what she wanted. A husband chosen for her, a life set for her, a house prepared for her. Bliss! And you would think this would be every girl's dream, but it wasn't. It wasn't her dream. Far from it in fact. Alissia's dream was to study, to learn, to be free, and maybe just maybe to be with the man that *she* loved. Yet this seemed like too much to ask. Maybe not for others, but for her. She lay there, promising herself she would find the courage to get up before being told to do so. *I need just a few more minutes. Just a little more time to myself. Just a few more moments with my thoughts.*

'You're getting married?' Lola was stunned. She couldn't believe it. Lola wasn't good at hiding her feelings. When she had something to say, she said it how it was. Often, she spoke before she thought. It could seem offensive to some, but it was actually quite refreshing to Alissia.

'Yeah… In a month. I don't have a choice…' Alissia was worried she had said too much. But she couldn't stop herself. She needed to tell someone. Lola had been a good friend to Alissia. The first time they'd met in front of the lecture hall, Alissia was intrigued by Lola's ways. Little did she know that day that Lola would soon become one of her closest friends, one of her only real friends.

'What do you mean you don't have a choice? There's always a choice. Even when you don't think there is, Alissia.'

'Yes, Alissia. There's always a choice.' Alissia didn't realise

Peter was standing behind them, listening in on their conversation. He wasn't supposed to find out yet. They had been getting close for a while now and on more than one occasion, Alissia found herself drawn to Peter. She knew she was walking on dangerous ground. Nothing could ever happen between them, no matter how much they both wanted it to, yet she couldn't help this attraction that kept drawing her in.

'You don't understand, Lola. I really wish you did but you don't. You don't know what it's like. It's not a choice. I don't have a choice in this matter. I never have.' Alissia was getting frustrated. She was beginning to forget she was talking to a friend. Her frustration was rising and quickly turning into anger. Her eyes were filling up. She didn't dare look at Peter whose own frustration could be felt from a mile.

'Then make me understand, Alissia. I'm here. I'm your friend and I'm not going anywhere. Talk to me.' Lola could feel how much Alissia needed a friend. Now was not the time to get offended. She could see Alissia's appreciation in her eyes. She ignored Peter's glaring look as he walked away, obviously hurt by this unexpected revelation. She would deal with him later.

And so, a month before her wedding, Alissia had started to properly confide in someone for the first time. She didn't leave out any details. There was no judgement in Lola's eyes, just friendship and love. Alissia had never been so grateful in all her life.

There's always a choice, even when you don't think there is.' The words that Lola had uttered that day had stuck with Alissia. She said them out loud in the hope that at some point, she would believe them.

Twenty minutes to go till your nightmare begins. Alissia could hear the voice in her head preparing her for the minutes, hours and days to come. And that's how Alissia spent the next twenty minutes of her life. These would be the last moments she would have to herself.

'Alissia, it's eight o'clock. Come on. You've had your rest. Time to get up and join us. There's a lot to do.' Alissia's mother was knocking as planned. Her big day had arrived and nothing was to go wrong.

Alissia didn't answer straight away. The thought of opening that door deflated her. She knew what was waiting on the other side of the door and she wasn't looking forward to any of it. *They'll all be there. All the women in the family. All waiting to congratulate me yet again on their big day.* Alissia was dying to think this out loud, but then she knew better than to do that.

'Come on, Alissia. What are you doing? We had a deal!'

'Yes, Mum. I'm coming.' Alissia knew this was the only option, at least for now.

'There you are! What were you doing? I've been up since five. Come on, Alissia. We have a lot to get through. This is your day. Let's get a move on.'

My day – ha! Alissia was worried her thoughts could be heard.

They proceeded to the living room. The house was of a very decent size, too decent almost. The living room alone could fit fifty people. Alissia should've appreciated it. She should've appreciated this giant house in Highgate, but she didn't. She longed to get away from it all.

'Surpriiiiiise!' There they all were, women and children. There they stood, all very excited, all fake as hell.

Alissia did her very best to smile. She tried very hard to appreciate this moment. She kept reminding herself that despite this whole situation, her mother had put a lot of effort into this day. But it wasn't her day. It was everyone else's day.

'Thank you,' Alissia muttered. This was dangerous. They were all staring at her, her mother included, yet she could feel the tears coming to the surface. This was not the time. *This was not the time.* *'There's always a choice.'* She could hear Lola's warm, reassuring voice.

'We'll be right back!' Her mother was about to take her away. This was not good. 'The buffet is ready. Enjoy!' Her mother's voice was high pitched. This was not good at all.

Her mother dragged her out by the arm. Alissia knew what was coming. Her heart was sinking by the second. Her mother took her back into her bedroom. Alissia panicked for a moment, wondering where she had left her phone, but then she remembered. It was tucked away. There was no way anyone would find it. Alissia had become quite good at hiding her belongings if she needed to.

'What do you think you're doing, young lady? I am warning you now. We have put a lot of time and effort into this wedding. We have spent an absolute fortune. We are surrounded by friends and family. Akil's mother is here, for goodness' sake. You know what you have to do, so pull yourself together, fast! Do not make me speak to your father, because if I have to, you know what will happen. You are behaving like a spoiled, ungrateful brat! This is not the time, nor the place. You have your entire life to be unhappy. So, I will say this once more. Pull yourself together and make us proud. You know what will happen if you don't. You've been warned before. Do you understand me, Alissia?' Alissia's eyes were filling with tears. She couldn't stop herself. 'Do you hear me, Alissia? I will not ask you again.'

'Yes, Mother. I hear you.' Alissia's voice was barely audible. Her confidence was at an all-time low. This was exactly what her mother was counting on.

'Good. Now, I'm going to give you two minutes to remember what is at stake here. And when you walk back in, you will appreciate everything that we are doing for you.' Her mother gave her a glacial look, making Alissia shudder with fear. There was no love in her mother's eyes. Alissia was beginning to realise what was at stake. Lola's words were fading fast and what she had felt for Peter was becoming a distant memory.

Her mother walked away, satisfied with their little conversation. And the next time that Alissia walked out, she was the perfect, dutiful daughter that she had been taught to be.

The entire day seemed to drag on like never before. Alissia was dying to check her phone. She had a feeling there were messages waiting for her. But she couldn't slip up. She couldn't afford to. She felt almost defeated. She could see that Akil's mother was waiting for her to make a mistake, just one. And in that moment, she was determined to prove that this would not be the case. Was it about making her own mother proud? Or was it about showing the community that she was worthy. *The community*. Every time she heard that dreaded word, she shuddered. There was no such thing as a community. They all loved to think there was, but there wasn't, because if something were to happen that could possibly go against the community's wishes, that was it. The so-called *community* would disappear. And yet there they were, all those women, eating, drinking and showing their so-called appreciation.

Alissia had so much rage in her heart. She had been dying to express it for years. She had tried once, but that night she had learned a very expensive and painful lesson. The engagement had just been announced. Ironically, Alissia hadn't been consulted. It had been assumed that spending a few hours with a man she barely knew was a sign she was ready to give herself to him. She knew she could never love him. Her heart had confirmed it the moment she had met him. Akil had taken a shine to Alissia. She didn't know how or why but he had. And he had spent the entire time staring at her. He must've thought he was showing her affection. He didn't know she was cringing inside. She couldn't afford to make it too obvious, considering their parents had an understanding. What was it that made her father so intent on marrying her off? Was it the fear she would meet someone herself outside of the community? Or was it the Mercedes Akil drove? Perhaps it was the terrifying thought of letting Alissia live a life that wasn't controlled entirely by him. Or maybe it was the five-bedroom house in Holland Park that he had pictured her in for so long.

'You know once we're married, you won't need to study or work, or anything like that.' Hang on, was he actually planning their future half an hour into the meal? 'I'll be there to support you. I can certainly afford to.' *Certainly* afford to? He was treading on thin ice already.

'That's sweet, but you don't need to worry about me. I'm on my way to something. And when I finish my bachelor's degree, I'm hoping to go further.' For a moment, she had forgotten who she was talking to. She was in love with her studies. It was her outlet, her personal treasure. Nobody could touch it.

'Well, honey, we can talk about that. No man wants to come between a woman and her hobbies.' Her *hobbies*? Her hobbies? Was he serious? Her eyes widened.

'Sorry? Did you just use the word hobby?'

'Hobby, interest, same difference.'

'Right...' Alissia could see there was no point in reasoning with this idiot. He was far too pompous and arrogant. A mummy's boy who had obviously been handed down Daddy's business.

When Alissia got home, having to stand Akil until the very last minute of their meeting—that's all she could call it—she couldn't hide her feelings any longer. She refused to.

'Look, if you like him, see where it can go. If you don't, be straight with your dad. What's the worst that can happen?' Lola was sweet. She was naive. She was a westerner. She wasn't wrong, but she was a westerner.

'Dad, I need to speak to you. It can't wait.' Alissia was feeling courageous.

Her father was in his office, busy at work. Alissia knew her next move wouldn't be a wise one, but she was feeling brave. It wasn't often that she felt brave. It was time to make the most of it.

'Be quick. I don't have time for this.'

'Father, I can't do it, I'm sorry. I can't marry Akil. I know you were hoping that tonight would go as planned, but it hasn't. I've tried. I really have, for you and Mother. This really isn't going to work. I'm sorry.'

Her father stayed quiet for a few moments and just for a second, Alissia was hopeful this was a good sign. It seemed like he was listening. And yet it was in that second that Alissia realised what she had done. Her father didn't say a word. He stood, staring at her coldly, waiting. Alissia's heart was thumping. She was starting to get scared. And that was it. That was all Alissia could remember of the night.

The next thing she knew, she was lying flat on the ground, unable to move. She knew she had been knocked unconscious.

This time, she had missed two weeks of her second year. She

had barely even left her room. Her books had been untouched. Her parents had won. In just over a year, Alissia would be marrying Akil.

When Peter had tried to contact Alissia, having begged her not to meet Akil in the first place, he hadn't had any luck. Alissia was in no fit state to answer the phone. She knew what he would say anyway. He would be hurt and upset. He just didn't understand that this was what was demanded of her. And as much as she loved Lola, her advice had got Alissia nowhere. They just didn't get it.

Alissia never answered the messages. She wasn't allowed to answer the phone. If her father caught her doing this, a few cracked ribs would be the least of her worries.

Alissia suddenly remembered where she was. Her mother had been calling her for the last two minutes and Alissia hadn't heard a thing.

'Alissia, darling? I know how excited you are but come on. It's time to say something to our dear family and friends!' Alissia knew that smile. It wasn't a smile at all. It was another warning.

Alissia rushed over, imagining the thousands of words she could utter in opposition to this whole farce. *I hate you. I hate all of you. I hate that you are all here, celebrating my funeral! I can't stand this. I won't stand it any longer. You think you are here to celebrate and toast my wedding when really you are just honouring my parents' wishes! I can't do this anymore!* Those were the thoughts that went through her mind as she stood up to say a few words in front of all these people she hardly knew, some of whom she couldn't stand.

'Erm... Thank you all for...' No, no, no. The tears were on their way back again, rushing to the surface. This was not the time. Please, please... Not now. 'Sorry. Thank you all for being here with me today to share these last moments.' These would be her last moments, wedding or no wedding. 'I'm… I'm just honoured to see you all here. If only you knew how strongly I feel about this all.' The message was there. It was up to everyone else to understand it as they saw fit. She was getting stronger. 'These moments are moments we will never get back. We must remember them for the right reasons and stay true to ourselves.' She couldn't stop herself. She was warning her mother at this point. 'Congratulations, Mother. Congratulations to us all!'

Idiots as they were, they were cheering and clapping on. They hadn't heard a word of what she was saying. And yet when she looked up at her mother, she knew. She knew her days were numbered. She was walking on very thin ice.

Her mother glared at her, all the while displaying her pride for all to see. The fakeness of it all made Alissia sick. How long were they going to keep up these appearances of the perfect family that they were not? For a lifetime probably.

Alissia stood down and walked over to her mother. This was tradition. An embrace from the bride's mother followed by the groom's mother. As she approached her mother, she could feel the tension mounting. She wasn't behaving as she was told. This would have consequences, not now, but later.

Akil's mother remained oblivious to the situation. She took Alissia into her arms. Akil's mother was a pro at this.

It was now one. They would soon begin the preparations for the ceremony happening later that day. Alissia should've been relieved that this part of the farce was over. Yet this was far from being the case. Just a day from now, Alissia would be married to a man she loathed. Her mother walked over and signalled to Alissia to start getting ready.

'You have an hour to prepare your things. The make-up and

hair team are coming over after this. Take a shower. Do what you need to do but be ready in an hour. Understood? Your father called. Everything has gone as planned on their end. Akil is very excited. Let's make sure it stays that way. Understood, Alissia?' And her mother walked off. She didn't await her daughter's reply. Probably because she knew. Or better still, she just didn't care. Another sign of the beauty of *honour*.

'Don't do this, Alissia. You can't make yourself love someone. People who say they can are lying. They're lying to you and they're lying to themselves. You know in your heart you don't want this. You are a thinker. You're passionate and determined. You've even impressed your tutors and we both know that doesn't happen every day. Remember what we talked about? Our dream? To think and to research. To sit in the most beautiful French cafés of Paris and share. Share our thoughts on Descartes, Spinoza and so many others. We promised each other, Alissia. I'm scared. I'm scared for you, my dear friend. Don't do this.' Alissia could see a tear in Lola's eye. She knew she had a friend for life there.

Alissia knew at least one text would be waiting for her. Lola was loyal. Peter, on the other hand, had stopped speaking to her and what could have been between them had ended when she announced she had no choice but to go through with this arrangement. He would never understand what was demanded of her. She'd hidden her phone where only she knew. This was the only way. If her family were to stumble on her phone, that would be it.

'I love you. Don't do it. Please. Please don't do it.' This was the first message sent this morning first thing. It went on. *'I haven't said it enough. I know I haven't. I've been so afraid. But you mean everything to me, Alissia. Lola's been such a good*

friend to you and what have I done? I've made things worse. I've shut down. I just couldn't handle it. I couldn't handle any of it. I felt so weak. I'm supposed to be there and protect you and I couldn't. I had to sit back and watch this whole situation unfold. I had to listen to you speaking about another man. I know you don't love him. Don't marry him, Alissia. Please don't marry him.' Alissia could feel herself breaking down. Why was Peter doing this now? Why couldn't he have said any of this before? She had given him the chance to. She had hinted at these growing feelings so many times. She had known from the start that their story could be beautiful. Yet, he had waited until today to say something. Up until now, he had shown resentment towards her.

She clicked off the message which she didn't have any time to digest because all she could see were more messages from Peter.

'I'm begging you, Alissia. Meet me. Please. Leave. Leave today. I know we're playing with fire here.' It was the first time he was using the pronoun *we*, almost like they made up a team. *'I've spoken to Lola. She can help us get away. She's thought it through, probably more than I have. But I can't let you do this, Alissia. I just can't. I love you.'*

'Please, Alissia. You're making a massive mistake. You know you are. And I'm afraid. I'm afraid for you. The bruises, the beatings, the abuse. It can't go on. Akil's not a gentleman. He won't take care of you. It wasn't so long ago you told us he raised his hand to you. If he's done it once, he'll do it again. I know they're your family, Alissia. But what kind of family locks their daughter away for days and weeks on end? What kind of family kicks you when you're down? What kind of family allows this to happen? Please, Alissia, meet me. Pack a bag and meet me.'

What was he doing? Why was he saying this now? What was

she supposed to do with this? She was meant to be getting ready. She couldn't do this right now. She loved him too. Of course she did. All she wanted was to leave. But she couldn't. Not right now. And then there it was, a message from her confidante.

'Alissia, I haven't slept all night. Peter's been in touch. The idiot's waited till now to tell you how he feels, as if that's what you need today.' Oh, how well she knew her! *'Listen, I can't stand by and watch you do this. I know you're scared and I know this is dangerous. But staying there is no less dangerous than taking a risk. Think about it, Alissia.'*

And then there they were again, what felt like a million messages from Peter. She didn't have time for this. If her family found out that she was even thinking about walking out, especially with another man, her life wouldn't be worth living. No, she had to get ready. At least for now, what would be, would be. And there it was, one final message.

'Alissia, last message for now I promise. I've spoken to someone. Don't worry. It was confidential. They're a charity. They can help us. They can help you get away. I know the pre-wedding ceremony starts at six and I remember you showing me the location. I don't have an eidetic memory for nothing. We'll be there, Alissia. We'll be at the venue before six. We'll figure this out. You don't need to do anything different for now. Get ready and don't let anything slip. Not even to your siblings, no matter how much you're dying to. Remember where their loyalties lie. We will get you out of there, Alissia, if it's the last thing we do. I promise.'

Lola wasn't one to break promises. Maybe, just maybe there was a glimmer of hope. Maybe her prayers would be answered. One way or another, she would be free.

Alissia came out of her room a few minutes early, to make sure that nobody suspected anything, dutiful daughter that she was. She pleasantly surprised her mother who was running around once again like a headless chicken. Everyone else had left. They were probably busy getting ready for the next part of her nightmare.

'Oh, Alissia, good you're here.' She noticed a slight grin on her mother's face. She was slowly winning her over. Her sister was nowhere to be seen, in her room probably, devastated at not being the centre of attention today.

The next three and a half hours were spent getting Alissia ready. She had never worn so much make-up in her entire life. Her head was being pulled in every direction known to man and she almost felt like she was watching herself in some kind of horror movie. But she felt strong. She was determined. And with true friends by her side, just maybe she could do this. All she had to do was play along for a little while longer. It sounded so easy. She knew that it would never be that simple, but she couldn't afford to think about it.

Her sister finally came out, a strange look on her face. Was it a look of empathy? Sympathy? Kindness? Love? These concepts were so strange to her these days, especially where her siblings were concerned. Alissia could see that she'd been crying. She'd stopped asking her sister what was wrong with her a long time ago, mostly because there was always something wrong. But today was different.

'What's wrong? Are you OK?' God, she could put on an act if she needed to. Alissia sometimes shocked herself.

'Look, Alissia, I know I haven't always been there for you, but I'm here now. I know you don't really want to do this. I can tell. You can deny it all you want, but I know.' Was this a trick?

She couldn't tell. Lola had warned her not to trust anyone, but this was her sister. She had to be able to trust her, surely.

'I'm OK, I guess. I won't deny this is hard, but I'm trying my best to get through the day.' Alissia was testing the waters.

'You're not OK. I can see that. You can say you are all you want, but we both know it's not true. I know you think you always have to act like the older one, but let me be your big sister for once. Look, I'll leave it there, but I'm here if you need me.'

'Wait...' Alissia was unsure. She could hear her mother's footsteps approaching. 'No, it's OK. I'm OK.'

'Don't worry, Alissia, I'll find you. I'll find you again and we'll talk.'

'OK...' Alissia was wary. She was glad she hadn't said anything.

She was left alone for the next five minutes. She used these wisely. She hurried to her room, picked up her phone and rushed to answer.

'Lola, thank you. From the bottom of my heart, thank you. I know you won't let me down. You're like the sister I never had. No matter what happens next, know I love you. X'

'Peter, I love you too. Of course I do. I can't believe you've waited till today to do something about it but I forgive you. How can I not? It's you. It's always been you. And when we are finally free, we can start that life we always dreamed about. I love you, always.'

Alissia knew she was taking a risk by doing this, but she sent off the messages and slid her phone under her bra. She made sure it was off and fully charged. She had to have some kind of security net.

Outside, a limousine was waiting. Her father and brother were in the car. This continued to be a family affair. Alissia

89

hadn't even looked in the mirror. She didn't care what she looked like. Being all dolled up didn't make her any more beautiful, even if that was what all those fake, superficial women of the community thought.

Alissia's mother stood in the corridor. 'Oh, my darling, you are a true vision.' *My darling? My darling?* What the hell was her mother going on about? Alissia didn't believe the act for a second. Had her sister said anything to her mother? Alissia didn't trust any of them.

Her sister followed her out.

'You really do look beautiful, big sis. I'm so happy for you.' Of course she was. Her mother was standing there. God forbid her sister ever think for herself. That was too much to ask.

Alissia could feel the anger and resentment coming back. Now was not the time. She was about to get in the car.

Take a deep breath, Alissia. Just take a deep breath and smile. The greeting from her parents was so different now, so different to what she had experienced until now. So different to all the days she had woken up after being locked in her room for a week. So different to the time she was busy finishing her 3000 word essay when her computer was smashed by her father in a moment of rage because she had dared to be tired at the table in front of Akil's parents, and so different to the day her brother had caught her on the phone and had told her father about this crime. Her father had wasted no time in making sure his daughter was punished. She remembered the smirk on her sister's face that day. Her sister had a field day watching her get punished for the umpteenth time.

Alissia got into the car with her brother and father. Her mother and sister followed on behind. The men dominated, of course.

90

'My daughter, my dutiful daughter, you look like a true lady today. A few words to the wise. Make sure you carry yourself like a lady before, during and after tonight's ceremony. Remember. It is the last one before the wedding tomorrow. Do not show us up in any way. Our honour is at stake here.' Of course it was. It was always about honour. Never about anything else.

She answered the only way she could at this point.

'Yes, Father. Don't worry. I will behave tonight.' That's all her father needed to know. Her brother was in the car which made giving anything away twice as dangerous.

'That's my girl.' *My girl*? She hadn't been his *girl* in years. She had probably never been his *girl*. Her sister on the other hand was the perfect daughter to a father like hers: spoilt yet obedient, superficial yet most obliging. She was the perfect fit.

Alissia was getting nervous. It had just gone half five and she knew that Lola and her army were waiting at the venue. They said they would be there for six. This really meant five. Alissia had no idea how this was going to pan out. She knew Lola would never let her down. And she knew, at least she hoped, that Peter would be there with her, to hold Alissia's hand, in some form at least.

The venue for this ceremony wasn't very far away. They'd been driving about twenty minutes which meant they would reach the venue soon. Alissia's father was busy communicating with her brother. He was probably preparing him to guard the night. Her brother was so naive. He liked to believe he was some kind of family martyr but he wasn't. He was just a lost little boy trying to prove himself constantly to his father. He had been seeking validation for years and he thought that by playing his father's sordid games, he would get it. Oh, how wrong he was.

The minute her brother set a foot wrong, that would be it. Yet she couldn't afford to worry about him right now. The only person she needed to worry about was herself. This sounded like a very selfish thought, but it was true. Each to their own.

They drove round the corner and as they approached the venue, Alissia got lost in thought for just a moment. For that one moment, she imagined what her new life could look like. A life with friends, books and freedom. The freedom to love, to study, to be. It was just too good to be true.

'Alissia! How many times do I need to call your name? We are here. Let's not keep our guests waiting.'

'Yes, Father. Could you give me a minute? Just a few seconds and I'll be out.' Her father warned Alissia with just a look. She couldn't quite tell what he was thinking but she knew now was not the time to play games.

Alissia looked around. She scanned the street around her. Were they here? She couldn't tell. She located a blue Ford Fiesta and wondered whether that was them. She had to trust that it was. Something was telling her this was the car.

It was customary for the mother to walk in first, to check on the guests and greet the mother of the groom. They were at a special table at the front of a large hall. Alissia's father accompanied Alissia into the hall, beaming with pride. *Honour*.

Akil was waiting at the entrance. As she entered the hall, everyone stood up to greet her. They were all cheering as if they were at the World Cup final. Alissia cringed at the thought of how fake she needed to be in that moment. 'Not for long…'

Akil greeted Alissia with open arms. They almost looked like the perfect couple. She knew otherwise but realised now wasn't the time. Alissia placed a kiss on Akil's cheek. She was keeping up the charade. *'Do not show us up.'* Her father's voice was beginning to haunt her.

Akil led Alissia to their table. They were to be seated by his parents. Her parents would soon join them. Her brother and sister were at the next table with aunts and uncles. Alissia looked over to her sister only to find her staring. She looked almost endearing in that moment. *Why did she ask me if I was OK today? She never does this...* Alissia couldn't work it out. She felt confused. Now was not the time to let her guard down, even though she was desperate to share her feelings with someone. *Don't be stupid, Alissia. Bide your time.*

Music was playing and Alissia was wondering when to make her next move. She knew a text from Lola would be waiting for her and the longer she left it, the more nervous she got. Disappearing suddenly would look suspicious. But going to the ladies surely wouldn't, not if she had someone with her.

'Time to take you up on your offer, sis.'

Alissia excused herself. Surely nobody could say anything about this. She signalled to her sister to join her. Her sister gladly obliged and followed her through to the ladies.

Alissia asked her sister to wait outside. Again, she agreed. This was strange. Her sister never willingly agreed to anything. But then, today was meant to be a *special day*, so maybe just maybe things were different.

'I won't be long.'

'OK, Alissia, take your time. Are you sure you don't want me to come in? I meant what I said earlier. I'm here.'

'I know... Thanks. But I'm fine!'

Alissia ran in and turned on her phone. 'Come on!' She was stressed. There was no way she was getting away with being in there for longer than just a few minutes, if that.

'Alissia, we are outside. Peter is keeping a lookout. There's

a blue Ford Fiesta a few seconds away from the venue.' She knew it! *'As soon as you can, make an excuse and meet me outside. I know you're nervous, scared even, but it will be worth it. I promise. We'll wait all night if we have to. Just join me outside as soon as you can get away.'*

How was Alissia supposed to walk out? Why had she stupidly brought her sister with her? It was almost like she knew her days were numbered and needed to feel close to her family, even just for a few moments.

'I'll try and get away as soon as I can. I don't know if I can do this but I want to. I want to more than you know. Please tell Peter I love him. And you. Lola, I can't wait. I can't believe this is happening. Is it really happening? OK, I will join you as soon as I can. I know I can't say goodbye. I know this has to end. It has to end tonight. I'd better go or my sister will suspect something. They all will. I'll see you soon, my dear friend.

Much love xxx'

Alissia put her phone down for a moment while she got herself together.

'Alissia, are you OK?' Her sister was calling. It was time to get back to the cavalry. Alissia rushed out without thinking.

'I'll join you in a moment, Alissia. I just need to freshen up myself.' Alissia didn't suspect anything at this point. She was in a hurry to get back to her husband *not-to-be*. Now was not the time to show herself up.

Akil acted like the perfect gentleman. He was nothing but affectionate and loving. Alissia cringed. She would give herself until the main course in twenty minutes before excusing herself from the table. She would need some air. Nothing serious. Just for a moment. She promised she would be back. They would insist but eventually, they would let her go. Her brother would try to follow her out but she would ask Akil to keep him busy. Akil would never refuse that offer. It wouldn't be a good look.

That's exactly what Alissia did. As everyone proceeded to begin their three-course meal, Alissia started to do the same, all the while locating her family and taking in her last moments with each one.

Alissia stood up as the main course was served. She looked down at Akil, discreetly letting him know she would disappear for a few minutes. Just for a moment, she sensed that he knew. She couldn't be sure so she ignored her instinct and walked out. There was no time to worry about uncertainties. As she left the hall as quietly as possible, she stopped suddenly. 'My phone! No, no, no, no, no. Where's my phone?' She knew it wasn't a good idea to go back to the ladies, but before she knew it, she was there. She desperately looked around. It had disappeared. Why wasn't it there? Who had taken it? She was really panicking now. 'OK, Alissia, think! What are you going to do? Run! Just run!' And she did.

She got to the door where she noticed her sister lurking around.

'Alissia, are you OK? What's wrong? Are you going somewhere?' Alissia knew it was game over. She didn't know what would happen next, but she knew she was trapped now.

'I'm fine! What are you doing here?' Alissia was trying to work out what was going on. She suspected something but she didn't know what. Her sister seemed so genuine.

'I came to check on you, silly. I just want to make sure you're OK. Shall we go back in? I think the speeches are coming up soon.'

'Erm… Yes, OK… Just give me a minute. I'll join you in just a moment.' Her sister walked away, more than happy to join the party again. This was Alissia's chance. Or so she thought.

'Alissia, come on!' Her brother barked. Alissia's heart sank. She had no way of contacting anyone and she knew she was being followed at every turn.

As she sat back down next to Akil, she could feel the tears streaming down her face. She didn't know why but she knew in her heart that the game was over for her. She just knew. She loved Lola and Peter so much for trying, but she knew the whole thing was too good to be true.

The rest of the evening became a blur. She didn't hear the speeches. She didn't care to. People kept approaching her, showing their appreciation and happiness. She could almost feel the envy coming out of them. She didn't care about that now. Her phone had disappeared. Her friends had no idea that she couldn't join them.

Alissia's parents were keeping a very close eye on her. She was being monitored from all corners. The night was soon to end and for some reason, Alissia felt like her life might just end as well.

The families separated for the night and Alissia was gently dragged back to the car. She bid goodbye to Akil, not knowing what this meant. She desperately looked out for the blue Ford, but it was gone. Alissia felt more alone than ever.

The way home was quieter than she had ever known it to be. Alissia knew that she was in trouble. She knew it was bad this time. She knew it wouldn't be just a beating she'd be getting.

Someone had picked up that phone. Someone knew. She couldn't believe that in the space of just a few minutes, her nightmare had woken up and was ready to laugh in her face. She was going to pay for this mistake. She knew she was.

The way back was unbearable. Nobody would look at her and when their eyes did meet, the look her father gave her was murderous.

It was late and there was no traffic, so getting home didn't take long, though in Alissia's mind, it had taken hours. As they reached the house, Alissia's father led her out of the car straight inside. Alissia never noticed the blue Ford. She was too busy obeying her father's orders whilst trying to hide her panic attack.

Her mother and sister were already there. Her father let Alissia go upstairs and get changed. Alissia thought about trying to climb out the window, but her sister had followed her.

'Alissia, you're in a lot of trouble. I don't think you'll get away with this one.' *This one?* Alissia thought. Her sister knew. 'I want to help, I really do. But what can I do? I'm just your baby sister.' She sensed sarcasm in her sister's voice. 'You're not thinking about slipping out, are you? You know you won't get very far.' That was enough!

'What is your problem? I don't need you to rub it in. I know this is bad. I know you won't help me. I don't need your help anyway. I never have. You're right. You are my little sister, my useless, jealous, spoiled little brat of a sister. I know you found the phone and I bet you couldn't wait to say something. You were so busy milking all the glory. It'll live on in your conscience. You don't think it now but it will. Mark my words.'

'Oh, whatever. Think what you like. You've never respected this family. Not really. You've always thought you were a cut above the rest of us. You've always looked down on me. You think that because I'm younger than you, that makes me an idiot.'

'That's not what makes you the idiot, trust me.' Alissia was fuming. She had to get it out. This may be her last chance. 'When we were younger, I tried. I tried everything. But you never

97

listened. You never showed you cared. And your priorities have been so misplaced. You should have cared about us, about me. But you never did. We are so different and the tragedy is that no one else can see it.'

'It's about honour, Alissia, this family's honour!'

'Honour? Honour? You don't know the meaning of the word. You make me sick. You walk around just waiting for everything to fall into your lap like you're entitled to it. You're constantly sucking up to Mum and Dad and just waiting for the day you can find someone to do everything for you. Well, let me tell you. You'll be waiting a long time. Sure, Mum and Dad will marry you off. They probably can't wait. But the only reason you're their favourite is because you continue to play this sick little game. Well, you know what? I live for my honour, not yours. And if you can't see that, well, then that's your problem. I don't need you, not anymore. There was a time when I did. That time is long gone.'

'Alissia…' Her sister was starting to feel what looked like guilt. Surely not…

'You've got me into serious trouble tonight, do you know that? And you've done it for all the wrong reasons. Earlier tonight, I actually thought you were genuine, only for a moment sure, but for that one moment, it felt good. It felt good to know that you actually had my back. Who was I kidding?'

'I'm…'

'You're what? Sorry? Don't be. What happens now is on me but just know that you had a part to play tonight and you played it perfectly. Congratulations!'

'Alissia, down now!' Her father was calling.

'I've got to go and face this. I wish things could've been different. I really do. At least, I used to. Goodbye, sis.'

'Me too... I'm sorry...' It was too late. Alissia was long gone. She hadn't heard her sister's apology.

Alissia got downstairs. The curtains were drawn and Akil was waiting along with her father. Alissia knew she had no choice but to take the consequences of her attempts to escape.

'You have disrespected this family's honour. You've disrespected Akil's honour. You are an absolute disgrace, Alissia. You don't deserve to be part of this family, or any other family for that matter.'

Akil joined in.

'What did you think? That I was just going to let you walk away with some white boy called Peter? That your friend Lola was going to save you? Nobody will save you now. Nobody. It's over, Alissia.'

Her father and Akil looked at each other for a moment. There was an agreement in their eyes.

As Alissia fell violently to the ground, she couldn't fight the beating she was getting. It was coming from all sides. She just wasn't strong enough to defend herself against these two very powerful men. Something inside her had given up.

With each weighted punch from Akil, Alissia could feel the pain of betrayal. He was punching so hard, she could feel her ribs breaking into pieces.

Her father's beating was the most poignant. He made sure his daughter could barely breathe. He didn't look at her as he forcefully inflicted pain in a way that she had never felt before. For just a moment, their eyes met. She thought she could see a tear streaming down her father's face. This was the very first time she had seen her father cry. It would be the very last. Alissia was too numb to respond and she shut her eyes. She could no longer look at her father. If he was disowning her, she was certainly disowning him back. She hoped that this single action would be a message to both Akil and her father, to her father especially.

In the distance, she could hear screams. She couldn't make out who was screaming or what was happening. Little did she know that Lola was beating the door down and that Peter was fighting his way in. They had called the police.

The beating must have lasted for all of ten minutes. That was what her life had been worth. Alissia hadn't tried to fight her father or Akil off. She had known the score from the moment she had remembered her phone, the very same phone her sister had found, gone through and handed to her father within minutes.

Alissia's life was beginning to waste away. Her sister was now sobbing in the next room, realising the seriousness of her own actions. She had never meant for any of this, not really. Her brother was busy trying hard not to show any emotion. He had thought about going in and stopping this carnage but he knew better than to do that. His own honour was on the line. As for her mother, she had gone to bed. She knew in her heart that she would have to live with the murder of her daughter for the rest of her life, but she was too proud and too afraid to stop what was happening. As a mother, she was proud, and as a woman, she was powerless. The denial was stronger than ever. Her daughter had after all been warned.

Alissia heard the police in the distance breaking down the door. Peter and Lola charged in hoping they weren't too late, knowing deep down that they hadn't been able to save their dear friend.

Alissia's father froze. He had murdered his own daughter, all in the name of honour. His actions were now beginning to sink in. Akil had made a run for it moments before. He had done right by his family and himself and did not need to be punished for this. His honour had been restored.

At 11.20 p.m., Alissia was rushed to hospital. Her friends had joined her in the ambulance, devastated. It was too late. The bleeding was internal and there was nothing the paramedics could do. Alissia died that night. She had been punished in the most brutal way one could imagine. Alissia's last thought had been the moment she had met Lola and Peter. This moment had changed her life and for this, she would be forever thankful.

Rest in peace, Alissia.

A Cruel Plight

'Now's not the time. She's upstairs working on a project for work. She's got a deadline in a week. You know how stressed she gets.' Jane thought she could hear her mum. Who was she speaking to?

'I know. It's a new job and we want her to do well. Of course we do. But you know we're going to have to tell her one of these days. We said we would. We said we'd keep our girls in the loop, Susan. They're not children anymore. Jane's twenty-five now.' Her dad sounded serious.

What were they talking about? Why were they being all secretive? What was this about? Jane walked into the living room.

'I was just making a cup of tea. Does anyone fancy one?' Jane was testing the waters. 'No? Sure? OK.' Jane walked back out.

When her parents thought she was out of ear shot, they continued their secret meeting.

'Do you think she heard anything?'

'I don't think so…' Jane could hear the uncertainty in her mum's voice.

'One of these days, she's gonna catch us out. I know it.' Her father seemed worried. 'On second thoughts, love, I will have that cup of tea!' He made sure she could hear that one.

'OK, Dad. I'll bring it through.' Jane was suspicious, but knew better than to probe when her parents were being all shifty.

They had a habit of doing this. They always thought they could get away with it, but they never did. She wasn't stupid. She would bring it up when they least expected. The trick was to catch one parent off guard and get them talking. 'Here you go, Dad. Two sugars, just the way you like it.'

'Thanks, love. You're a gem. Don't tell your mother, but your tea's always been my favourite.' Her dad always had a way of putting a smile on his daughter's face. She couldn't help but feel love for him every time.

Jane decided to forget the conversation she'd overheard for now. This was not to say she wouldn't do some digging at some point, but now was not the time.

'How's the work project going, love?'

'It's not really, Dad... I'm hoping that a break'll do me good. It's not going anywhere right now and it's due in in the morning.'

'Don't you worry, love. Take a break, have a biscuit or two and remember you're the best they've got. Take a break for now.'

'You sure you're OK, Dad? You're looking a little tired. Should I be worried?'

'No, love. You know me! I'm fine. Don't worry your pretty little self. You get back to work and impress the socks off those bosses.'

'Do you promise, Dad? Do you promise there's nothing you're not telling me?' There was a double entendre there. Jane was hoping her father would understand the hidden meaning behind her questions. Maybe he did. Maybe he didn't. It seemed though, that he wasn't giving anything away.

'I'm fine, love, honestly. I promise. Now get back to work and stop worrying about your old dad.'

'You're not old, Dad!' Jane kissed him on the cheek and disappeared back upstairs.

'Cat, do you ever get the feeling there's something Mum and Dad aren't telling us?' Jane had decided to quiz her little sister. There was more than one place to look.

'How do you mean? I don't think so… I mean I know Mum and Dad can be a bit secretive, but we've always told each other everything, haven't we?' Her sister was busy thinking and answering the question at the same time. 'Anyway, what makes you think there's something they're not telling us?'

'Nothing… I just caught them having a conversation the other day, and when I walked in, they pretty much stopped talking. They looked shifty as hell. It was weird. I think they're hiding something.'

'You know they're like that sometimes. It's usually nothing to do with us though.'

'I know. But this time was different. This time, they looked like they were hiding something, something they obviously didn't want me to know.'

'Really? Are you sure? That really doesn't sound like them.'

'And then Dad made up some excuse about a doctor's appointment.'

'I wonder what that's about. I hope there's nothing wrong. Surely we would know if there was.'

'You'd think so.' Jane had been stirring her sister's tea for about five minutes. 'Oh, sorry! Here you are.'

'Thanks, sis. Look, I don't think we have anything to worry about, but if we do, we'll find out soon enough.'

'Let's hope so.'

Her sister walked out of the kitchen. She was in revision mode. Her final exams were coming up. She couldn't burden her sister like this now. Still, Jane wasn't feeling very reassured. She had a feeling something was wrong. She was usually right.

Something was telling her not to drop this. She knew she wouldn't get anything out of her parents, especially not her mum.

Her mum was quite a secretive person. She never shared too much. She always made a point of showing that some things couldn't be shared with children. Her and her sister weren't children though. They hadn't been children for some time. Still, that didn't matter to her mum, who would rather deal with her problems alone most of the time. This left Jane frustrated. She knew she could help her mum, but her mum was too stubborn to ask for help. Her dad on the other hand was usually like an open book. She could share anything with her dad.

Growing up, she had lived in fear of her mum but never of her dad. One of her earliest memories was opening the chest of drawers in her parents' bedroom and finding a load of photographs and letters. She was too young to understand what that was about. She didn't recognise the people in the photographs, nor could she read the letters. She was only four. But when her mum walked in, you'd think she'd broken into a bank. Jane had been worried to approach her mum for days after that. It was her dad who had come in and told Jane not to worry. Mummy would calm down and be right as rain in no time. *What a strange expression.* There was no rain when she looked outside. But if her dad had said it, he'd meant it. She never did find out why her mum was so angry that day.

There was another time when Jane had walked in on a phone conversation her mum was having. She remembered her mum's face when she'd caught her daughter listening in on this very private moment. She'd never run to her bedroom so fast, petrified of what was about to happen next. Again, her dad had been the one to come and find her, gently dragging his daughter downstairs.

After those two incidents, Jane hadn't dared ask her mum so many questions, afraid of her mum's reaction, even now. Some things never changed.

Jane had this nagging feeling there was something her parents were hiding from her. She just couldn't work out what it was. She didn't know where to start. Her sister obviously didn't know anything. They were close and Jane knew her sister wasn't lying.

Her phone rang and she snapped out of her thoughts.

'Jane, you OK? I've been tryna call you for the last half hour.' Poor Eric was worried about her.

'Have you? I'm sorry! I didn't even hear my phone.' She quickly checked. There were about five missed calls. When Eric worried, he dialled.

'We were meant to have lunch, remember? Does the word anniversary ring a bell?'

'Oh, God, I'm sorry! Is it really the ninth today?' God, she felt bad. She knew Eric had gone to a lot of trouble. He always did. 'I'm really sorry. My mind's been elsewhere. You know I'd never knowingly let you down. Can I make it up to you?'

'I s'pose...' Eric was quite good at forgiving Jane. This wasn't the first time.

'Great! Meet me for dinner. I promise I'll make it up to you.' Jane knew she had some making up to do.

'If you can fit me in,' he joked. Jane was quite busy these days and it seemed that her career often came first. Why would tonight be any different?

'Don't be like that. I promise it's not a work thing. I'll explain everything tonight.'

'I'll look forward to it.'

'Oh, yes, you will!' And that was it. He was gone. Just as

well. She had a few calls to make.

'You OK, love?' Jane's dad crept up on her and made her jump.

'Dad, you scared me! Are you OK?'

'I'm fine, love. It's the funniest thing. I came in here looking for something, but I can't remember what it is now. Can't have been very important.' Her dad looked slightly disorientated.

'Come and sit down, Dad. You're looking a little flustered.' She got him a glass of water.

'Am I? Oh, don't worry, love. I'll be fine. You get back to work. You've got that project coming up, remember?'

'That was yesterday, Dad. And thanks to our little chat, I aced it!'

'Oh, that's great, love. I knew you would.' He got up to walk away.

'Are you sure you're OK, Dad? Maybe I should stay with you.'

'Oh, that would be nice.' He never usually responded so casually. Usually, her dad would be pushing her out the door right now. Something wasn't right.

'That's settled. I'll cook us a little meal. Mum's working late tonight. It'll be just you and me.'

'OK, love. Sounds good.'

Eric would kill her if she cancelled again. She'd done this so many times before. She knew he'd end up hating her. But her dad came first. Surely, he'd understand...

'Eric, I'm so sorry to do this to you. Don't hate me! I'm worried about my dad. He's not himself. I'm going to stay in and look after him tonight. I promise I'll make it up to you soon. Love you xxx'

It took her a few minutes to send the message. She was

dreading the response, especially as it only took Eric a few seconds to send it.

'*OK, no worries.*' Oh God, he was really angry! She thought maybe a second text would do the trick.

'*You must really hate me. I'm sorry. I promise I'll make this up to you. Please don't hate me, Eric. Love you loads xxx*'

Nothing came back. She decided to leave it for now and get back to her dad.

She walked into the living room to find her dad staring into space. This wasn't like him. He wasn't usually so subdued.

'Dad, are you OK? You've forgotten to turn on the TV. Countdown's on in a minute. Let me get the remote for you.'

'Thanks, love.' He turned on the TV and hit the third channel.

'It's not on ITV, Dad. It's on Channel 4. Honestly, where's your head at these days?' Jane was endeared by her dad's naivety.

'Oh, of course it is! Sorry, love. What was I thinking?'

'Should I be worried about something? Do you want me to get you anything?'

'Don't be silly! Now get us a cup of tea and stop fussing.' That was more like it. Jane smiled to herself, looking back to check her dad's next move. 'Come on, love!' Jane ran out of the living room, knowing her dad had sussed her out.

She didn't hear the kettle boil straight away. For just a moment, she was lost in thought. Maybe it was a good idea to have a word with her mum. Maybe she'd noticed something too. Or maybe her mum would deny there was anything wrong. She was good at that. Whenever Jane broached a subject her mum didn't want to address, she somehow found a way to divert her attention, or to walk out of the room. It was almost a talent of her mum's. She wouldn't let her get away with this one though, especially not if it was serious.

'Where's that cup of tea, love? I'm parched!' Her dad very quickly brought her back to reality.

'Sorry, Dad, just give me a minute.'

'OK, love. Take your time.' Her dad was so relaxed. It wasn't often that he stressed her out. Everything could always wait. Granted, this was sometimes the case with the bills too, but he had such a positive outlook on life. It was actually quite refreshing.

She checked her phone. Eric hadn't been in touch. He must've been really angry this time. She felt bad. She knew his patience was wearing thin. They'd been together for four years now. They'd met at uni, on their marketing course. It was the passion and fire he'd fallen for, and it was his natural ability to charm anyone round with his pitches that got her every time. In theory, they were a force to be reckoned with. In practice, they were slowly drifting apart, especially since she'd started her new job. He hadn't directly begrudged her anything, but she knew the resentment was building up. She should've been doing everything she could to work on their relationship and to stop them from drifting apart, but she wasn't working hard enough.

Anyway, now wasn't the time to worry about this. Countdown awaited her! It was Friday afternoon. She wasn't at work and she was about to spend some quality time with her dear dad. Eric could wait.

'Here you go, Dad. Sorry about that. I was a million miles away.'

Her dad didn't say a word. For just a moment, she caught him staring into space. He was starting to worry her. Surely if there was something to worry about, she would know. But then she hadn't been at home enough these past months. She hadn't

109

had the chance to keep a close enough eye on her dad. Every time they did spend some time together, he seemed fine. Not today though. Something wasn't right.

'Dad, you know that doctor's appointment you mentioned? Anything I should be worried about?'

'Oh no, love. Your mother went and booked that one. For some reason, she's a bit worried about me. I told her not to fuss, but you know what she's like when she gets an idea into her head.' Her mum hadn't mentioned anything about this, and her dad was so casual about it.

'What kind of appointment, Dad?'

'Just a general check-up, I think. You know your mum deals with this stuff.'

Apparently so. Why hadn't her mum mentioned anything? It was so typical of her, always trying to deal with everything on her own, as if Jane and Cat were too young to understand. It was so frustrating.

'Ooooh, look at those letters. How's that contestant going to get out of that one?' Her dad suddenly seemed so disconnected, like they hadn't just had that conversation. 'What did you say this programme's called? It's a good one. Good choice, love.'

'It's Countdown, Dad. You watch this every day, remember? You've never missed one. That's why we've still got so many videos lying around! They should really be DVDs now, Dad, but then I haven't won that one yet.' Surely her dad remembered Countdown. What was that about?

'Countdown! I'll have to remember that name.'

Jane walked out for a moment. She couldn't get her dad's faraway look out of her mind. What was her mum doing booking an appointment and not telling anyone about it? Her mum was due back soon, so hopefully she could shed some light on what

110

was going on here.

'Mum, can I ask you something?' They were in the kitchen and Jane was bracing herself for an answer she wasn't ready to hear.

'Yes, of course you can, Jane. Hang on, let me just get the shopping in the hallway. I'll be right back.' This was so typical of her mum, always stalling when there was something she didn't want to answer.

Jane waited a few minutes. Her mum was taking her sweet time. Of course she was. She knew what was coming.

'Right, I'm back. What's up, darling?' Her tone was calm. This was hopefully a good sign.

'Mum, I'm a little worried about Dad. He doesn't seem himself. Earlier, we put on Countdown and he pressed the wrong channel. Then, when we started watching it, he couldn't remember what he was watching. It was like he was seeing his favourite programme for the first time. I kept catching him staring into space. It's as if he wasn't with me today. And then he mentioned something about an appointment that you'd booked for him. But you haven't said anything, so I'm not sure what he was talking about.' OK, she'd got it out. It was up to her mum now to keep the conversation going.

'Oh, the appointment. It's nothing to worry about. Just a general check-up. Your father's over fifty. It's standard practice. Nothing out of the ordinary.' Her mum was in denial mode again. Jane couldn't afford to get upset. Her mum would never open up if she did.

'Mum, is everything OK? I know something's up. Come on, this is me you're talking to. It's OK. You can tell me. I know I haven't been around much lately. I'm sorry. But I'm here.' She walked over to her mum cautiously. She had to approach this one softly.

'No, honestly, darling…'

'Mum, you're crying. What's happened?'

'Nothing, hon…' Her mum couldn't hold in the tears any longer. They were streaming down her face at one hundred miles an hour. Jane caught her mum who could barely stand at this point.

'Mum, it's OK. Whatever it is, we can deal with it as a family. I can be around more. I can take time off. Come on, Mum, tell me.'

Her mum recomposed herself. It took her a few moments to calm down. Jane knew she was about to confess.

'It's your father. He's been, well, he hasn't been himself for a while. He's been forgetting things.' Jane knew she couldn't cut her mum off at this point. It was time to sit down and listen. 'Take the other day. I told him to go out and get the paper for me. He came back with a pint of milk instead. He couldn't remember what he'd gone out for, but had bought the milk just in case. And the Countdown episode, well, it's not the first time. He can't remember a lot of what we watch. And then there's your aunt, your dad's sister. She called the other day. Your father couldn't remember who he was speaking to. She didn't pick up on anything. You know your father. He's nothing if not a good actor. But I could tell. There was a look in his eye.' It was that same look she'd caught earlier today. 'Anyway, I've booked him an appointment for next Tuesday. Not a word to Cat, do you understand? You know how important these A-levels are to her. She's hoping to get into Cambridge. Now isn't the time to crush that dream.'

'Understood.' Jane wasn't altogether comfortable with keeping this from her sister. But her mum had a point. Now

112

wasn't the time.

'Right, now not a word to your father. Get the salad out and get chopping!' Her mum picked herself up within seconds and Jane knew she was putting an end to their conversation.

Jane followed her mum's instructions, knowing how tough this conversation must've been for her. She wondered how long her mum had felt this way. She had no right to say anything, especially as she hadn't picked up on her dad's condition. All those times he must've been hiding his feelings of confusion and of how lost he was. She couldn't imagine her dad being in this state. *But then, children often try to ignore their parents getting old. They like to keep them young.* Her father wasn't old though. He was only fifty-three. He was even two years younger than her mum. What did that say?

Jane knew her mum wouldn't want her at the appointment just yet. She asked anyway.

'Mum, do you want me to come with you on Tuesday, for moral support? I could wait outside. I don't mind.'

'Oh no, darling. Don't worry your little self. We'll be fine.' She wasn't little anymore though. She was twenty-five. Why did her mum keep saying this? Now wasn't the time to ask.

'OK, well, if you change your mind, let me know. I'm sure they'll give me the morning off.'

'It'll be fine. Honestly. You just get back to work and keep doing what you do best.' Her mum was definitely in denial. She'd called the practice and booked the appointment, but there was denial in her voice.

'Right, anyone need the magic touch? Can I do anything for my two favourite ladies?' Her dad must've sensed they'd been talking about him. He was a little too eager to help.

'Dad, what about Cat? Your third favourite lady?' Jane knew

how touchy Cat was about these things, so she often made a point of correcting her dad.

'Three? Oh right, yes, of course! Little Cat. Anyway, can I help?' It was quickly becoming a family affair.

'Sure, Brian. You peel the potatoes. They're over there. And the peeler's in that drawer. Do you know the one I'm talking about?'

'I'm not daft, Susan! Honestly, your mother, Jane. She cracks me up.' Her dad was back.

Jane helped set the table and clear up after the meal, all the while realising just how much she'd neglected her family. Feelings of guilt were starting to creep in at the thought of having abandoned her family. Now was the time to make up for all those months of absence. Work couldn't come first anymore. She needed to set her priorities straight. She still lived at home and if anything, it had to stay this way for now.

Jane and Eric had talked about moving in together. They were both on 30k+ now. They could certainly afford to. But she'd have to put her plans to one side for now. Her dad had to come first.

Jane lay in bed that night, wide awake. She couldn't sleep. Tomorrow was Saturday and she was due at work at eight. All employees had to be in one Saturday a month. It was part of the contract. She'd have to go in. Now was not the time to skive off, especially if she was going to be asking for more time off soon.

Two in the morning, God! It was going to be a long one. Eric still hadn't replied. He obviously wasn't in the mood to hear from her. She thought it best to give him some time, a cooling off period as it were. If he wasn't in touch by Sunday night, she'd nag him. For now, she'd leave him to it.

The weekend was proving to be a long one. No word from

Eric. A couple more days till her dad's appointment. People usually did a little light research beforehand, not Jane though. She had watched countless friends and colleagues diagnose themselves with terminal illnesses, depression and countless other conditions that weren't worth mentioning. They were absolutely devastated every single time. She couldn't handle the pressure. That's what doctors were there for, to diagnose their patients. Who was she to do their work?

Tuesday morning finally arrived and Jane made her mum promise she'd call once they got home.

'Promise me, Mum. I know what you're like. You always say you will and then I don't hear from you. I know you're strong. I know you've got this. But you're not calling me for yourself. You're doing it for the child that loves you and that can take it, OK?'

'I promise, darling. I will. Now, stop fussing and go to work. We'll be fine. That is, if your dad ever comes out of the bathroom. You'd think he's going to the casino!' Jane's dad always did this. Whenever he was going somewhere, he would take ages. He'd drive his family up the wall! On this occasion though, Jane could forgive him anything.

'Dad, I'm off!'

'OK, love. You have a good day. What time's the appointment, Susan?'

'10:15, for the tenth time.' Jane was relieved her dad didn't hear that last bit.

She set off. She was at work by nine and at her desk under a minute later. Her boss hated when anyone was late. They would never hear the end of it!

Jane spent all morning checking her phone. Surely her mum would call soon. She'd promised! And for once, she'd actually

115

kept her promise. It was eleven-thirty when the phone rang. Jane couldn't care less what anyone thought. The boss wouldn't like it, but then, he wasn't the boss of her life!

'Hello, Mum, is everything OK?' She could hear panic in her mum's voice.

'They want to send your dad for more tests. They're a little worried. The GP wouldn't let me go in with him. Apparently he wanted to see him without me. I didn't like leaving your father alone with him. He came out all frazzled, almost like he'd done something wrong. The GP called me in afterwards. He said he didn't want to diagnose him there and then, so he would be sending him for more thorough tests. They want to send him to a neurologist and do an MRI scan. The GP didn't want to tell me but I forced it out of him.'

'What do you mean? Forced what out of him? What did he say?'

'He said… Oh God… He said your dad might have a form of dementia.'

'Dementia? What? But he's too young! Mum, that can't be true, surely.'

'That's what I said. The doctor said he couldn't tell me any more. He was going to make sure that the referral was done right away. He said we should hear back in the next forty-eight hours.'

'Mum, do you want me to come home? I can leave now. I'll be home in an hour.'

'Oh no, darling, don't you worry about that. I've told the office I'm taking the rest of the day off. I'll stay home with your father. You get back to work and I'll see you tonight.'

'Are you sure, Mum? I can leave now. It doesn't feel right being at work when all this is going on.'

'There's nothing we can do right now. You get back to work

and I'll see you later. I love you, darling. See you at home.' And that was that. Her mum had hung up. She often did when she could feel herself about to cry.

Dementia? Dementia? What form of dementia? Surely that couldn't be right. Jane couldn't take it in. Now wasn't the time to take it in. Her mum would kill her if she left work. No, now was not the time to think about this. Now was not the time to have a breakdown at work around people she didn't really care about and who didn't really care about her.

She got stuck into work all afternoon and left at five o'clock on the dot. So there were a few unfinished files. Her team wouldn't be too happy about that but to hell with them. If they needed it done, they were welcome to get to it themselves!

It had just gone six o'clock when Jane got home. Her mum and dad were sat in the living room, watching the news. Her mum had dozed off, probably exhausted from the news she'd received earlier on.

Her dad looked up and smiled.

'Hello, love. You're home. It's not like you to be early. Has something happened? Shall I make you a cup of tea?'

'No, no, don't be silly, Dad. I just wanted to come home, that's all. And a cup of tea sounds great. You always know what to do.' She put her arms round her dad, tighter than ever before. She was trying not to let her dad see her cry.

'Love, what's wrong?'

'Oh nothing, Dad. Must just be that time of the month. That cup of tea sounds fab. Thanks, Dad.'

'All right, love. Your wish is my command.'

As her father walked away, he seemed smaller somehow, more frail than she would have liked. Yet now was not the time to lose it. He was the same dad she'd always known. Nothing had changed. At least, she tried to believe that. She had no choice.

'Oh, you're back, darling.' Her mum was waking up. 'You're not usually back at this time. Thanks for coming home.'

'Oh, Mum, you don't need to thank me.' Jane was beginning to realise the effect of her absence. 'You'd better get used to it. I'm going to be home a lot more. Dad's just gone to make me a cup of tea. You'd think he was on top of the world.'

Jane and her mum looked at each other and for a second, they could feel the love pouring out of each other. They weren't used to this. It was a strange feeling, but one Jane could definitely get used to.

'Right, I'd better go and check on your dad, make sure the kitchen's still in one piece. It's good to have you home, darling.'

'It's good to be home, Mum.' Jane felt like for the first time in ages, she really was home and she intended to keep it that way. Her mum wasn't usually this loving. Jane thought she should make the most of these moments. She had a feeling they wouldn't be around forever.

Within twenty-four hours, the next appointments had been booked. A scan to start with and further memory tests, finishing with an appointment with the neurologist. All of this in the space of under two weeks. There was barely enough time to take in the situation. A week ago, Jane thought that her life was completely normal. Work, home, her relationship, her dad, and now she was questioning her own sanity. Was all this even real? A form of dementia? The GP hadn't wanted to say any more. That couldn't be a good sign. The fact that he had said anything at all was bad.

Jane's dad didn't know what was happening, not really. He had always sort of just gone with the flow. Nothing had changed there. To think that her dad didn't know what was going on around him was probably for the best. Yet that was the scariest part. The lack of control. Her dad had no control over what was happening and the family was powerless to stop it. Cat was completely oblivious. She often caught her sister and mum in conversation. Yet she would never quite catch what was going on. Jane was trying her best not to lie to her sister, but it wasn't easy. She had to keep reminding herself that her sister's future was at stake. So she kept quiet and followed orders. As for her mum, she would often catch her in a daze. It was like all that energy she once had had disappeared. She was deflated. It was up to Jane to keep the family ship above water.

Her father went to each appointment without making a fuss. Maybe he knew deep down that he was deteriorating. He'd just never say it. All part of a father's pride.

'Come on, Brian. We're going to be late. Jane, you get to work. You don't want to be late either. Cat, finish your breakfast! You've got your English exam this morning. Honestly, you'd think we had all the time in the world these days.' Time was exactly what they didn't have.

Jane's mum hadn't wanted her daughter at any of the appointments. She'd promised to call her every time and update her. They would only really know anything in a week during the appointment with the neurologist. That was the big one. Her mum was right. Up until that point, there was nothing Jane could do. She'd left a ton of messages on Eric's phone but he hadn't got back to her. She'd vowed to go and see him in the next few days, or at least give him a call. She'd wanted to. It wasn't that she hadn't. She just couldn't bring herself to tell him what was really going on. That would mean she had to admit the truth of what was going on to herself, and she wasn't fully ready for that yet. Maybe it was selfish of her. He deserved some kind of explanation at the very least, and he would get one, just not yet.

The next few days were long and hard. Jane was hardly getting any work done. She knew she wouldn't get away with it for too long. She was on probation and the firm she worked at was fast-paced. You were expected to give your all, all of the time. Prior to this whole situation, she'd thrived on deadlines and pressure. But somehow these last weeks, she'd felt disconnected from it all. Her passion for marketing was quickly disappearing and she was feeling increasingly out of touch with the corporate world. All she longed for the moment she left the house was to get back and be with her dad. She called home about five times a day. She knew she was probably suffocating her parents with this new found concern but she had to check on them.

It was on the morning of the appointment with the neurologist that her manager walked into her office to have a chat and 'check in'. Her mum hadn't let her call in sick and drive them to the hospital. She was to go to work and that was that.

'Morning, Jane, I hope I'm not disturbing you. I just wanted to have a quick word.'

'No, no, of course not. Come on in.' This wasn't a good sign. The head tilt said it all.

'I'm not big on these chats so I'll get straight to the point. We're worried about your performance. A few people have complained.' *We*? *A few people*? She knew exactly who he was talking about. Mandy had never liked Jane. Jane was young, vibrant and determined. Mandy was older and well, past her prime. She hadn't liked Jane since the moment she'd walked in and she'd made her feelings quite clear on a number of occasions.

'Oh, right...'

'Jane, I like you, I really do. You're fast, motivated and most of the time, you're at the top of your game. But lately, your performance has dropped. It's nearly cost us a client, and you know we can't afford to lose our clients, especially those who have been with us for such a long time. I don't want to have to let you go. I really don't.' God, it really was a nasty game.

'I understand, Paul. I know you're only doing your job. Things haven't been easy at home lately and I admit I've been struggling to keep my mind on work.'

'Listen, Jane. You really don't have to go into detail. It's none of my business. I'm going to suggest that you take a leave of absence. You've got a good two weeks left haven't you and it's already October. So why don't you finish the day and take some time to re-evaluate. Get back to the Jane we all know and love.'

'Actually, Paul. That wouldn't be such a bad idea. Thanks.'

'OK, Jane. Listen, we'll keep this little chat between the two of us for now. Just come back alive and kicking, OK? And in the meantime, keep in touch.'

'I will. Thanks, Paul.' As he walked out of her office, Jane burst into tears. The pressure really was starting to get to her.

She knew she owed Paul one good day's work, Jane style. So, she did as he said and finished the day, tying up as many loose ends as she could. Anything that had been left untouched, she emailed to her team. She got a text from her mum. It didn't say much, just that they'd talk when she got home, which was probably best. She knew it wasn't good news, but then in all honesty, she'd known that all along.

When Jane got home that evening, she decided to be completely honest with her mum. In the past, she had been known to bend the truth slightly if she felt it was necessary. But now was not the time to be selfish.

'Hello, darling Dad. Is Mum around?'

'Oh, hello, love. Where have you been?' Her dad had a look of concern on his face.

'Nowhere special, Dad. You know, the usual.' Jane gave her dad a kiss on the forehead, just as he had always done when she was young.

'Isn't that project due in, love? I'm happy to be your guinea pig anytime.'

'What project, Dad? Oh, that project! No, Dad. That one was due in weeks ago. You were my guinea pig, remember? And thanks to your talents, I aced it.' Jane was trying hard not to let her dad see the tears in her eyes. 'I'll be right back, Dad.' He didn't respond. He must've been exhausted from the day's events.

Jane walked into the kitchen, forgetting to put her bag down. When she got to the kitchen, she saw her mum looking very distressed.

'Mum? Are you OK? I'm home. I need to tell you something, Mum. Mum?' It took her mum a moment to realise her daughter had walked in.

'Oh yes, sorry, darling. I was a million miles away.'

'Mum, Paul, my manager's given me some time off. He said I could do with being at home for a while.' Her mum didn't need to know why. At least not for now.

'Oh, that's good of him.'

'Mum?' It wasn't like her mum to dismiss something like this.

'Yes, darling. Sorry. I'm just not quite with it.' Her mum looked shattered.

'I know something's up, Mum. Tell me. What did the neurologist say? Mum?'

'He said… He said that your father's not very well.'

'Not very well? What do you mean, not very well?'

'Well, you see, your father's been diagnosed with early-onset Alzheimer's disease.'

'Early-onset Alzheimer's disease? What? Are they sure?'

'Quite sure, darling. They've run all the necessary tests. Your father tried but he didn't quite pass the memory tests. He tried really hard.' Susan couldn't look at Jane. The heartache was real.

'But...'

Just then, Cat walked in light as a feather.

'What's going on here? Has someone died?' Cat had just finished her last exam. Now wasn't the time. 'What time's dinner? Can I call Katie? I really wanna know how she did in science.'

'Yes, of course, you can. Take your time. I was thinking we might have takeout tonight. Anything you like.'

'Steady on, Mum! I haven't got the results back yet!' Cat couldn't believe her luck. 'On second thoughts, Mum, forget what I just said. Can we do pizza? Sis, I'll let you do the honours.' And just like that, Cat was gone.

Jane walked over to her mum, who was barely holding it together.

'Mum, I'm scared. I'm really scared.'

'So am I, darling... So am I.'

Jane grabbed her mum and hugged her tighter than ever before. She wished she could freeze this precious moment with her mum.

'We're going to need to stick together. This is going to be hard.'

'I know, Mum. I know. One day at a time, eh? Let me go and sit with Dad for a while and you order the pizza. We'll let Cat be a teenager for a bit longer. We'll tell her soon.'

'OK, darling. Whatever you say.'

'Love you, Mum.'

'Love you, Jane.' They hadn't said those words in a while. Jane realised just how much they meant to her. She walked out and went to join her dad in the living room and just for a while, they sat.

Jane knew she wouldn't get these moments back. She knew now that this was the beginning of the end for her dad. Things would never be the same again. She was losing him, her dear old dad.

'I love you, Dad…'

'Love you too, love. Now what's for dinner? I'm starving!'

'Eric? It's me. I'm sorry I didn't call sooner.' He'd answered which was a start. 'How have you been? I've missed you…' Now wasn't the time to play hard to get.

'Hi, Jane.' She could sense the cold tone in his voice.

'I wanted to call before now. Something's happened. I really need to talk to you.'

'Right. Well look, I'm a little busy at the moment.' He wasn't giving anything away.

'Of course you are. I'm sorry. I'll let you get on.'

'No, look, it's fine. What's going on?'

'I want to tell you. I really want to talk about it. Just not over the phone.' She was getting emotional.

'Look, if you're going to waste my time, forget it, Jane.'

'No, Eric, please. Look, Dad's not well. We got his test results today.' She was trying hard to breathe between words. God this was tough.

'Brian? What do you mean? Is he not well?' Eric was

softening up. He'd always been a fan of Jane's dad. Who wasn't?

'Yeah, he's... He's been diagnosed with an illness.'

'What? Christ, Jane! Is it serious?' The tone of contempt had quickly been replaced with concern for her dad. She tried not to read too much into it.

'Yes, it's... Oh, I can't even say it. It's just awful.' The anger within her was rising. God this was unfair!

'OK look, do you want me to come over? I know it's late.' He was offering. She knew this was a big step after what she'd put him through.

'Eric, I'd really love that. I don't wanna impose.'

'Impose? Come on, Jane. How long have we known each other? Give me half an hour.' And then he was gone.

She couldn't believe that after all this time, after having messed him around and left him hanging so many times, he was still willing to come over. Jane was one lucky woman and in that moment, she was finally beginning to realise just how lucky she was.

Jane saw a missed call on her phone and heard a light knock at the door. It was half eleven and Eric didn't want to wake the family. Jane rushed to the door.

'Eric, you're here.' She jumped on him, for a moment forgetting they were on shaky ground.

Eric hugged her back. He was and had always been a true gentleman. He knew that Jane needed him. Now was not the time to be funny with her.

'You going to keep me out in the cold?'

'Oh, yes, sorry. Come in.' Jane led Eric into the living room. 'Let me get you a drink. Help you warm up.'

'Thanks, Jane.' And there it was. The tone of reproach, very subtle yet very clear. Jane knew she had no right to say anything.

She had to take it and she would, for as long as she needed to.

'Here you go. I know it's late, but never too late for a glass of wine.'

'Thanks, Jane. So, what's happening? You sounded so distressed on the phone.'

'Yeah, sorry about that. It's been a tough few weeks. It's been like a whirlwind. I feel like I don't even remember half of it to be honest.'

'You said it was serious on the phone.' His look of concern was so genuine. All she wanted was to be close to him. She knew she didn't have that right just yet.

'Yes, it is. Dad's been… Well, he's been forgetting things.'

'What do you mean, Jane? Everyone forgets, don't they?'

'That's what I thought, but it's more than that. It's Dad's look. Sometimes, I'll catch him staring into space. If you ask him what's wrong, he'll make up some excuse or make a joke of the situation, but I know there's something wrong. And the other day, Countdown was on and he couldn't remember the channel. That's never happened before.'

'He probably wasn't paying attention. Surely that doesn't mean anything.'

'But it does, Eric. It means there's something wrong, something really wrong.' Jane was getting frustrated now and she couldn't quite work out why. Eric knew better than to get offended.

'OK… So have you taken him to a doctor?'

'Mum has. She's taken charge. The GP referred Dad to the local hospital and he's had tests done. Mum took him to the neurologist today.'

'The neurologist…?' It was starting to sink in.

'Dad's been diagnosed with…' Jane took a breath. 'Sorry.

He's been diagnosed with early-onset Alzheimer's disease.' She couldn't believe she'd actually said the words out loud to another person. But then, Eric wasn't just anyone. He was Eric.

'Jeez, Jane. I had no idea. I'm sorry.'

'That's the worst bit, Eric. Neither did I. Can you believe it's taken me this long to realise there's something wrong with my dad? My dad? I've been so busy with work and worrying about what now seems meaningless, that I never picked up on this until very recently.'

'The day you cancelled dinner. It makes sense now. Oh God, Jane. And I haven't been getting back to you. I'm sorry, sweetheart. I really am.'

'No, don't do that. Don't be nice to me. I don't deserve it.' Jane's frustration was almost turning into self-pity. 'I've been so worried about myself all this time, so wrapped up in my career, that I haven't noticed what's been staring me in the face all along.' This wasn't just about her dad and she knew it. 'You've been here, waiting for me to wake up, and what have I done? I've taken it all for granted. I've taken you for granted! And now my dad's ill, I mean really ill, and I'm losing the most precious person in my life.' Jane let her face sink into her lap.

'You haven't lost me, not yet anyway. We've just... drifted I guess. But we haven't sunk, at least not yet.'

'But, Eric, I've been such a cow to you.'

'No, you haven't. You just let the money and the fame get to you for a while. Well, maybe not the fame, but as good as.'

'I did, didn't I... You know they've put me on leave. My performance isn't quite up to scratch.'

'What? You mean you haven't been married to work this week?' Eric grinned.

'I deserve that one. No, it seems I haven't. Let's call it a trial separation, though with the way things are going, it seems the divorce may be impending.' Jane laughed for the first time in a while.

'Look, tell you what. Why don't you get some rest and we'll talk tomorrow? I've gotta get back. I have an early start in the morning. I'm meeting a potential new client and you know how it is. I've got to charm the pants off her.'

'Oh, so it's a she?'

'Jealous are we?'

'Is it OK if I am?' Jane was inching closer to Eric.

'I'm thinking it is. Anyway, why don't I come over when I'm done? It might be late in the day, but we can hang out, the three of us, you, me and Brian. And if you're lucky, I might even stay over for dinner.'

'Do you know what, Eric? That would be just great. And listen, I want you to know, I love you. I'm sorry if I haven't said it enough, especially lately, but I do. I really do. And I promise you that things are going to change.' She looked deeply into Eric's eyes as she said the words.

'I've missed you, you know. See you tomorrow.' He gave Jane what felt like the kiss of her life and just like that, he was gone.

Jane knew that they had a tough road ahead of them, but somehow, Eric had managed to make her see yet again that everything was going to be OK. She didn't know how he did it, but he managed to every time without fail.

'I love you xxx.' It was never too late to start again and tonight had proven that. He would get her message when he got in and hopefully, he would know that she really did love him.

All of two minutes after she'd sent the message, she got one back. So, he did still love her. For the first time in a while, she could go to sleep knowing that life made some kind of sense.

Jane had decided that staying home didn't mean she got to sleep in. She had decided on a new routine. Her mum had to get back to work, and now that she had time to spare, her dad could have a new stay-at-home buddy.

'Mum, is it OK if Eric has dinner with us tonight? He came round for a bit last night and wanted to come back and spend some time with Dad.'

'So, you've told him?'

'I'm sorry, Mum. I had to. Our relationship is hanging on by a thread as it is. And anyway, he's always really liked Dad. It's only fair, isn't it?'

'Did you tell him Cat doesn't know?'

'Don't worry about that. I'll make sure he doesn't say a word.'

'Right, good. I'm sure your father will look forward to his visit. I won't be back late. I'll get away as soon as I can.'

'Stop stressing, Mum. You get to work. I've got this.' She heard the door shut behind her mum.

'Dad, it's just you and me today! Cat's out and Mum's at work. What do you fancy doing? Dad? You OK?'

'Right, love. I'd better head out. I'll be late for work myself if I don't get off. What time's that train?'

'Work? Dad, no. You haven't worked at that firm for two years now. Remember? You're home with me today.'

'But I'll be late, love. Sorry, I really would love to stay and keep you company but I've got to get off.' He grabbed his coat. He was still wearing his slippers.

'Dad, come on. Let's go and sit down.'

'I can't, love. Didn't you hear me? I've got to go! You get to school. You'll be late yourself at this rate and we don't need

129

another detention. Your mum'll go mad.'

'Detention? Dad, what are you talking about?' Jane was starting to stress. 'I won't be in detention. I'm twenty-five, Dad. Now come on. Let's go and sit down. Give me your coat.'

Jane could see how restless her dad was getting. She knew she wasn't helping, but he wasn't making any sense. Hopefully, if she insisted enough, he would listen.

'Dad, come on. Let's get a cup of tea and sit down.'

'That's enough! I've got to go.' Her dad rushed out the door, his coat half on. Jane rushed out behind him.

'Dad, where are you going? It's freezing!' Jane didn't know what to do. She'd never seen him like this. It was like he was in some kind of trance. He just couldn't hear anything his daughter was telling him. 'Dad, please. Come back!'

'Who are you calling dad? I'm not your dad. Get off me! I don't know you.'

'Dad, it's me, Jane.'

'Jane? Who's Jane?' She couldn't believe what she was hearing. They were out in the cold, just the two of them. Jane didn't get the chance to get her own coat. Her dad was too far out the door.

'Dad, please…'

'I told you to stop calling me that. I don't know you. Get off me!'

The next thing she knew, her dad was walking out into the road. Cars were beeping left, right and centre. Jane was panicking now.

'Dad, watch out!' A car broke suddenly, and Brian fell to the ground. 'Dad, are you OK? Oh God!' She rushed over and knelt down to pick him up.

The driver got out. He didn't look best pleased.

'What the hell was that? Are you OK? You want to look where you're going mate!'

'I'm so sorry. He's not well. I'm really sorry.'

'Where are we, love?' He was coming back to her.

'Dad, it's OK. You fell. You're all right. Let's go home, Dad, OK?' She tried her hardest not to cry. What had just happened? What had become of her dad? She could see the driver calming down.

'Look, can I help? Drive you anywhere? Is your dad going to be OK?'

'I don't think he is. But it's OK, thank you. I'm really so sorry.'

'No harm done, I s'pose.' He got back into his car and drove off.

'Dad, come on. Let's go home.'

'Who are you, love? Have we met before?' He didn't recognise her. She was starting to understand it was best to play along.

'Believe it or not, we have. We met twenty-five years ago.' She picked him up and slowly they walked home.

'Twenty-five years ago? Gosh, I must've been handsome then.'

'Oh, you still are! So very handsome.'

'My name's Brian, by the way.'

'Jane. Nice to meet you, Brian!' And that's how slowly but surely, Jane began to educate herself. This was the first time that her dad had got ready for work since the start of his condition, but it wouldn't be the last.

Over the next weeks, she realised she was slowly beginning to lose the father she had known her entire life. It was devastating and completely out of her control. What a cruel disease they were dealing with.

'Mum. I've made a decision. I'm quitting.' They were back in the kitchen. Somehow, it had become their conference room.

'Quitting? What are you talking about?'

'Today's my last day off. They want me back in tomorrow. I can't face it. And what's more I don't want to. I have a dad who needs me. He really needs us, Mum. You didn't see him that day. It was awful. He's not coping.'

'That was a one-off, darling. He's going to be OK. I've reduced my hours at the office.'

'Mum, it's not going to be OK. I'm sorry but it's not. He won't cope on his own. Trust me on this one. I've spoken to a few people, nurses and other people who are going through something similar, caring for a loved one. What happened the other week will happen again, and next time we might not be so lucky. If we're not home with him, God only knows what Dad'll do. He's not even really recognising me anymore.'

'We've got a while before he deteriorates, darling. Besides, you've got a career that you can't afford to put on hold.'

'Mum, you're not hearing me. I've written my letter of resignation. I'm handing in my notice. I've spoken to Eric. He's going to help out more as well. It'll do Dad good to have a male figure around. Granted, he doesn't know who the hell Eric is anymore, but what can you do?'

'Jane, are you sure about this?' Her mum wasn't putting up much of a fight. Jane could see the look of relief on her mum's face.

'I'm sure. And listen. It's time we told Cat. Her exams have been over for a while now. The longer we choose to keep this from her, the more she'll hate us for it. We're telling her when

132

she gets back.'

'But…'

'Mum, no arguments. We aren't children anymore. It's time we pulled together as a family.'

'You know, they're really going to miss you at that firm.'

'Oh, I'm not so sure about that!'

Her sister came through the door just as their conversation had ended. Speak of the devil. Jane took Cat and her mum upstairs. Jane did the talking. Cat sobbed her heart out and excused herself.

'It's OK, Mum. She needs some space. It's understandable.'

That night, Eric came round. They had dinner as a family and everyone made an effort, except her dad who seemed restless.

'Brian, are you OK?' Eric looked at Jane with concern.

'Who are you?'

'It's me, Eric. Your daughter Jane's boyfriend. Remember?'

'But I don't have a daughter!'

'Dad, it's me, Jane, your eldest.' Jane knew she had to be gentle. She couldn't ambush him like last time.

'Jane? Who's Jane? This isn't my house! What am I even doing here? I've got to go. I've got to get to work.'

'What's going on? What's happening? Dad?' Cat was getting very emotional. She was panicking.

'Stop calling me that! I'm not your dad!' His anger was mounting. He was beginning to fight off his family. 'Get off me! Didn't you hear me? I've got to go!'

'Brian, it's eleven o'clock, dear. It's time for bed, not work.' His wife's soothing voice was beginning to calm him down. And then he got up again. This time, he forgot his coat altogether. They knew they had to start playing along, and fast.

'Brian, why don't I take you to work? I've got to get to work myself.' Eric was thinking on his feet.

'Erm… right. Do you know where I work?' He had a look of suspicion on his face.

'Of course I do. I've been there before, remember?' Eric was getting good at this game.

'Right… come on then. Let's go.' Jane could see her dad was slowly lowering his guard. She couldn't have been more grateful to Eric if she'd tried. She got in the car with her dad and boyfriend and they drove off. She made sure to text her mum, let her know everything was OK.

They must've driven around for what felt like hours. She'd need to be at the office tomorrow to hand in her resignation. She would ask to work off her last weeks from home. If they refused, to hell with them!

They got home around one in the morning. Her mum was waiting up, completely terrified.

'Well, young man. How much do I owe you for the ride?' Her dad was coming back to them again.

'Let's put it on your tab, shall we?' Even Eric had to hide his emotion at this point. What had happened to the funny, confident and kind man he had once known? He turned to Jane. 'Listen, you go in with your dad. I'll head off. I don't think it's a good idea for me to stay round tonight. I'll call you tomorrow. Good luck at work!'

'Are you sure? I'm so sorry about this. Thank you so much for tonight. You're a hero.'

'You've never called me that before.'

'What are you two whispering about?' Her dad was wary. They couldn't risk another scene tonight.

'Jane was just paying me the fair, Brian.'

'Oh right. Thanks, dear.'

It had been a very long night. One of many to come.

The next few months had been tough. Jane had quit work to become her dad's full-time carer. Her mum had gone part-time. She couldn't afford to quit just yet. Jane's dad was beginning to deteriorate fast.

Jane took her dad to a group once a week. While she informed herself and spoke to other carers, sharing stories and advice, her dad shared his time with other patients. Most weeks, he would agree to go, but some weeks, he would resist. Jane was lucky her dad never became physically violent. It had never been his style. Yet he had shown his frustration and anger in other ways. He would often say hurtful and spiteful things to his daughters and his wife, especially if the mood took him. Most of the time, they could cope with it. Yet there were times when they would really need to pull together and remind each other that this wasn't their Brian. This was... Well, that part was hard to understand. What an evil disease. The only solace they took was in the fact that he was never quite aware of what he was doing. This was something that every carer agreed on. And in many ways, the lack of awareness was a godsend to those who were ill, yet a nightmare for those around them.

'Dad, are you ready to go?' She could tell today just wasn't going to be their day.

'Go? Go where? This is where I live!'

'No, Dad. This is the hospital. We visit a few times a week but this isn't home.'

He was refusing to get in the car, determined to win this one. Oh, how stubborn he had become!

'Right, well, I don't know about you, but I'm going back in.'

She sighed at the thought of having to follow him in yet again. But what other choice did she have?

Luckily, he was quite popular with the nurses. He'd managed to charm them from day one.

'Right, come on, Brian! Get in the car.' The nurses were good. They were very good. Brian got in the car and Jane drove off, thanking them a thousand times for their endless patience.

'Where do you want to go, Dad?'

'It's funny you keep calling me that. I have a daughter you know? She's in marketing.' Jane knew who he was talking about. This wasn't the first time he had confused her.

'Oh, really?' She managed to smile even though this was killing her inside.

'Oh yes, she's a right shark! They're all terrified of her. Actually, don't say anything, but she scares me sometimes too!'

'Oh, really? Jane burst out laughing. 'She really does sound scary, your daughter. Have you told her any of this?'

'Oh, I wouldn't dare! No, she's better off thinking I'm the boss.'

'Yeah, you're right. You wouldn't want to anger the beast.'

'Exactly! What did you say your name was again?'

'Oh erm… Jane.'

'Fancy that. Just like my daughter.'

It was moments like this one that Jane would go on to remember later in life. It was also these moments that hurt the most.

Later that year, Jane's sister went on to study English at Cambridge. She was so proud of her. Cat came back to visit most weekends. Every time she did, she could see her dad was getting worse. The goodbyes were always heart-breaking.

Jane's mum continued to work part-time shifts at the office

and when her mum was home, they took turns. Jane had managed to find a part-time job working from home. It didn't pay half as much, but Jane was fine with this. She'd realised where her priorities lay and she was grateful for the opportunity.

Eric sometimes did the night shift. He now had two jobs. One at his firm where he had been promoted to team manager and a night job, driving Jane's dad around.

Her dad's condition was deteriorating and Jane wondered how long they could go on like this. But she had learnt to live in the moment, one day at a time.

Jane cared for her dad until his last moments, all the while reminding herself that deep down, he knew who she was: Jane, his beloved daughter, always.

Betrayal

She looked around her and realised she was alone. She didn't know how she had got here or where in God's name she had been. She stopped for a few minutes, wondering. She wondered what had happened, why she couldn't remember anything. Had she blocked out the past months? Was she living a nightmare? She just didn't know.

There was a knock at the door. She didn't dare answer it. Who could that be? She didn't remember inviting anyone round. But then, there was so much she didn't. Should she answer the door? Should she take that risk? She stood motionless, as the knock hardened. She felt like she had been there for hours before the knock suddenly stopped. There she stood waiting, petrified, alone.

The phone rang. Was it her mobile phone or the landline? Nobody really used landlines anymore. So why was it ringing? Who could it be? As it dawned on her that she was alone in the house, her heart began to thump, beating louder and faster with every passing second.

She didn't dare answer the phone. What would she say? Who could it be? Was she expecting anyone? She just couldn't remember. For the life of her, she could not remember a single thing.

She began to pace around the room, mumbling to herself. Where had she been the night before? Was anyone with her? Was she alone? She thought about calling someone, but who? Who could she trust to tell her the truth? Was there anyone? No, there was nobody. She didn't even trust herself.

She ran to the living room and opened the door. Were her belongings still there? What was she wearing last night? *Think! Come on! Think!*

She looked down and found her bag where it always was. Her keys were there and so was her wallet. So, she had brought them home. How had she got home though? She couldn't work it out. How had she even got in? She had her keys so she must have let herself in somehow. She was consumed with emotion, guilt, confusion, shame and above all, loss. She felt lost. She had to keep reminding herself she was home. Yet no matter how many times she did, she found it hard to believe.

Had she been out? Had she met any friends? How had the night ended? If only she could remember. She threw her keys down in a rage. She was furious. How could this happen to her? She was always so responsible. She was so organised. In fact, she was the organiser wherever she went. Friends, work, home. Everything had to be organised or she just couldn't cope. What the hell had happened that night then? Was there no explanation? Surely there had to be an explanation. She felt to scream.

She wasn't going to find the answers like this. Her therapist had taught her to count to ten. Count to ten and breathe, which was what she did. She counted and counted until her thoughts finally started to calm themselves.

She would find out what had happened to her that night, even if it was the last thing she would ever do. 'You can do this,' she whispered. And just as she knelt down to pick up her keys, the knock at the door resumed...

'Where is she?' He was getting really worried now. He hadn't heard from her for the past two days. It wasn't like her to be this distant. Sure, they had their ups and downs. They hadn't been on the best of terms lately. But he had put that down to their relationship. It was nothing. It was just the way they were. One minute, they were head over heels in love and the next, they couldn't stand the sight of each other.

'Pick up after yourself! You never do.' He could hear her from a mile away sometimes, almost like she was watching him, watching his every move. But surely that wasn't why she hadn't made contact. Even after a screaming match, he would get a text the next day. She was a woman, so of course she was angry. And of course, he needed to remember that her calmness was always passive aggressive. Women!

But this was different. He hadn't heard from her. He had rung around, but no luck. Nobody had heard anything for over twenty-four hours. He was beginning to worry.

He thought back to that time they had argued. It was far from the only argument they had ever had, but this one had been different. She had touched a nerve. It had stung and she had hit him where it hurt. He didn't want to go into it. He remembered hating her that day. He had never hated her before. *There's a thin line between love and hate.* And that day, he'd crossed over.

Where could she be though? And why wasn't she getting in touch. They knew the deal. You never make the other person worry this much, no matter how much you want to punish them. You let them stew for a while, sure. That's fine, an unspoken rule almost. But beyond that? No. You just don't do this to someone you claim to love. And every other time, she hadn't. He hated to admit it, but he was worried.

Was it time to call the old bill? The God almighty police? What would they do? He wasn't being funny but seriously, what would they do? He remembered calling them once before after the disappearance of his younger brother. What was it they had said? 'We all know what you're like in your early twenties. He's probably just gone out on the pull and had a few too many.' Gone out on the pull? Were they serious? He remembered the smug look the officer had given him before leaving. That encounter had left a bitter taste in his mouth.

'They're not all like that you know. Have a little faith.' And she was right. They weren't. But now wasn't the time to reminisce. He didn't want to think about what state his brother was in when they had found him. OK, he had gone out on the pull, but that was beside the point. And anyway, would she really want him to ring the police? Dial that dreaded number, only to be told he would need to call back? And in that time, he could be holding up the line. She could be trying to reach him.

Maybe she was trying to reach him right now. Where was his phone? He paced up and down, trying to locate it, not realising it was in his pocket all along. She could drive him absolutely insane, even when she wasn't there.

Where the hell was she? He had absolutely no idea. He went to the kitchen to drink a glass of water. *What's water going to do?* Now wasn't the time to drink. He had to keep a level head.

Where was she? No matter how many times he repeated these words to himself, he just couldn't for the life of him work it out. Jason was beginning to get really scared...

Amy was starting to panic now. Who was at the door? Who was ringing? Should she answer either? Considering she couldn't remember what the hell had happened, she followed her instinct. *Come on, Amy – think! What happened last night? Where were you? How did you end up back here?*

141

Was she with anyone? Did she call anyone? *Think, Amy, think!* And yet the more she pressured herself to remember, the less she felt she knew.

She had always lived the way she had been taught, by the book. She had never stepped a foot wrong. You couldn't count that time she was caught smoking in the girls' toilets. That wasn't her fault. She was pressured. She was only thirteen. Nor could you include the time where her first boyfriend had caught her cheating. She was so unhappy. She had suspected him for months. All she could see was her need for revenge. So, she did it. She went to a club that night and drank. She drank her troubles away, and the next thing she knew, she was waking up next to some stranger she'd picked up, as Michael looked on. It was at that moment she realised he had never cheated. She would never forget the look of devastation in his eyes. She had broken his heart.

She had never felt such shame. And that was when she vowed never ever to do this again. Another reason she didn't drink. It was almost like she didn't know what she was capable of after a glass of wine. Most people can handle their drink. The worst they might do is dance on a table or make the call of shame to Mum and Dad. Not her, not Amy. She paid for her mistakes. *Every single time.*

Had she drunk last night? What had possessed her? What was she thinking? She couldn't for the life of her remember. Why couldn't she remember?

It was no use going round in circles like this. It wouldn't change anything. Tears streamed down her face. She couldn't stop herself. She couldn't believe it. Was she losing complete control of her life?

Amy never cried. She hadn't cried in years. The last time she had cried was the day her dad had walked out on her mum and her. That day, she had cried her eyes out. She was eleven. After that, her mum had stopped functioning, spending days on end in bed. She would never forget that fateful day. That day, she came home to see her mum off her face, barely recognisable. She was thirteen. She had tried everything to help her mum. But she just couldn't get through. No matter what she did, she couldn't get through.

She would come home to see things missing. What had happened to her diamond necklace? The one her grandma had left her. Or the stereo she had been saving up for? She was fifteen. She was fifteen the day she realised her mum wouldn't be around to look after her little girl for much longer. That was the day she left home, never to look back.

She was twenty-seven now. Twenty-seven and alone. Alone in her thoughts, alone in her flat, alone in her life. She was all alone and there was nothing she could do about it.

Where was Jason when you needed him? Men! She knew he would never step up. Why couldn't he understand that when a woman says she doesn't need you, it doesn't actually mean she doesn't need you? It means she bloody well does need you.

'Where are you, Jason?' Was he even thinking about her? They argued so much these days that the odd doubt did creep in. *One day, he will meet someone. And you will be nothing more than a cheap fling. Just a meaningless fling.*

She wanted to believe that what they had was more than just a physical connection, but she didn't feel loved. That was it. She felt unloved. Unloved and alone.

'That's your trouble, Amy. You only hear what you want to hear. Why won't you listen to me for just once in your life? I'm here, aren't I? Is that not enough for you? Am I not enough for you? I don't know if I can keep doing this! Jesus!'

And then he'd walked out. Walked out and just left her there. She should've said something, anything. She knew she should've said something. But the words just wouldn't come out. And anyway, what was the point? He'd just end up leaving her. Everyone did. Her dad, her mum, her grandma and now Jason. Who was she to stop him? If that was what he wanted.

It had been two days since that conversation. She hadn't written since. They had this unspoken rule. No matter how angry they were, they wrote. This rule always applied. But when someone tells you they can't do it anymore, surely that says it all. So, she hadn't called him. She had decided to break that rule.

She looked up. The phone had stopped ringing. There was no knock at the door. Just silence. Had she just imagined what had happened? Was this all some kind of bittersweet dream? Or a sick joke? God only knew.

No, it couldn't not be real. She'd pinched herself to check. She was very much awake.

'Hang on. What in God's name am I wearing?' It wasn't like her to wear what she could only call a belt. She used to look down on women who wore cheap tat. And yet, there she was.

She went to the mirror. 'What the hell am I wearing?' Her red shirt was missing the top three buttons. She never wore red. She thought it made her look cheap, kind of like the time she'd walked in to find her mum entertaining. Her mum had been wearing red that day too. The closer she looked, the more she could feel her mum's lingering presence. She felt the tears in her eyes as her mind painfully travelled back to it. She hadn't thought about that day in years. So why today? What was dragging her back down?

She picked up the nearest object she could find and before

144

she knew it, the mirror was smashed to pieces. And as she threw the vase to the floor, she let herself drop to the ground, sobbing in the process.

'This can't be happening to me!'

Jason picked up the phone and started calling round again. What good was it standing there, imagining the worst? He was a man. He couldn't just sit there moping around. He was a man and as a man, he was used to trying to fix situations. Apparently, this wasn't always what women needed. Every time Amy had a problem, a work problem or a social issue, she would talk to Jason about it. She would rant and go on for ages. Jason would listen, all the while thinking of solutions and possible ways to fix the problem. Amy couldn't stand this. 'I hate the way you're always trying to fix me. Is that what I asked of you? No! It isn't. All I need is for you to listen. Just do it. Just once.'

Whatever, he would think. No matter how much he tried, he would never understand women. Were men even designed to know what women wanted? Probably not. God's little joke.

Amy wasn't here to complain this time. He would've given anything to hear her complain. Anything. Yet if she did turn up, she wouldn't need to know this little fact.

Jason dialled like a maniac. He spent the next hours dialling away and asking around, trying everyone he knew and everyone he thought she knew. Someone would know where she was or what she was doing. He left as many messages as he could in the hope that someone would get back to him soon.

He even tried Sheryl, her best friend. He really didn't want to have to but this was more important. There were priorities in life. He'd argued with Sheryl not so long ago. She'd interfered one too many times. Sheryl was the type to interfere. It was almost like a part-time job for her. Amy would have to remind him that she was doing it for the right reasons. She was just trying to help. It was her way of showing she cared. She must've cared a lot the amount of times he got it. But then, why did Amy have to go and share every little detail of their relationship? So, he was a bit of a ladies' man before meeting Amy. What did that have to do with Sheryl? It wasn't like he had ever chatted her up! She wasn't his type anyway.

Sheryl had a problem with the way they'd met in the first place. Amy was on a bit of a rampage at the time. She wasn't doing too well. She was between jobs and feeling a lack of attention. It was only after Jason got to know Amy that he saw what lack of control could do to her.

Fair enough. When he first met Amy at a bar and chatted her up, she was just another woman, a very attractive woman at that. The fact that she wasn't wearing much was a bonus. An easy target. Your typical woman waiting to be chatted up. She was clearly up for it. And they played right into each other's hands. It didn't take long for him to take her home, not before getting her number in case he was ever in the mood for round two. He had woken up the next morning to an empty room. No note. Just the lingering scent of her perfume.

He went back to the bar a few times that week. She was nowhere to be seen. Obviously a one-off. One of those one-night stands that sticks out. That week, he couldn't get her off his mind. His mates teased him for days on end. There was something different about him. Almost as if he was actually falling for her. How could he fall for a woman he didn't know? A woman he'd only slept with once? Well, three times if he was being accurate.

After a week or so, he'd given in. He'd actually dialled her number. This was not something he did ordinarily. He was not in the habit of calling women back. He didn't need that kind of hassle and anyway, his pride was at stake. This time though, he didn't mind taking the hit. He would never hear the end of it from his mates, but he was hoping it was worth it.

Amy didn't remember him at first. She was probably playing hard to get. The ladies didn't usually. Usually, he was in there from the moment he walked into their lives. He had to admit he was intrigued. That night, she'd seemed completely up for it. He didn't even need to ask for her number. She seemed like a completely different person over the phone. Luckily for her, this just made him want to get to know her even more.

He invited her out to dinner, an invitation which she reluctantly accepted. They would meet at the Gordon Ramsay restaurant at eight and he would wine and dine her then.

Of course, Sheryl didn't remember any of this. She was so busy thinking about his chat-up lines and womanising ways, except he hadn't gone near any other women since meeting Amy. He had given up the single lad's life the moment he'd fallen for Amy, which was pretty much straight away. Sheryl always had to stick her nose in where it wasn't wanted. She didn't trust him. He knew that. But she didn't need to make it so obvious.

It was time to put aside his pride once more and call her. He couldn't help but feel a sense of relief when she didn't pick up. He left her a message, the first in a long line of messages he had been sending out for what felt like hours.

Amy reached for her phone. She could think of only one person she could trust herself enough to ring. Sheryl had been there before. They'd been friends for years. In moments of desperation, she was the only one Amy could turn to.

The phone rang and Sheryl soon answered. She could hear

desperation in Amy's voice. She knew something was wrong.

'What's happened? Jason's just called. I didn't pick up. He left a message. He sounded desperate. What's going on?'

Amy broke down in tears. Sheryl's heart sank. Amy had done it again. Another night out. Another blackout.

Sheryl knew she had to keep Amy calm. Step one of the friendship rulebook. Keep your friend calm in a crisis.

'I don't know what's happened, Sheryl. I'm scared. I don't know how I got home. I don't recognise the clothes I'm wearing. I don't even recognise myself right now. What have I done? Did I call you last night? Please say I called you.' Amy was panting down the phone.

'You didn't call me, sweetie. I wish you had. Talk me through what's happened. What can you remember?' Sheryl was hoping for some sort of explanation. Any explanation was better than no explanation.

'That's just it. I don't know. I don't remember a thing. I feel like I'm reliving a nightmare here. It's déjà vu, isn't it? I promised myself I would never do this again. I promised *you* I would never do this again. I've let you down, haven't I, Sheryl? I've really let you down this time.'

'Don't be stupid, Amy. Of course, you haven't let me down. Let's not go there now. Don't start punishing yourself. It's not healthy. Take a deep breath and listen to me. Jason's just called. He—'

Amy cut her off. 'Jason? Jason doesn't care about me. He doesn't give a damn. You were right about him. You were spot on. I should never have gone there. I should never have trusted myself around him. Where is he now, eh? Where's Jason now?'

'He's worried sick, Ames. He's been ringing around, trying to find you. Check your phone. There must be tons of missed calls. He's terrified of losing you. Jason loves you, Amy. I never thought I would hear myself say it, but he loves you. He'd do anything for you.'

'Yeah, right! Come on, Sheryl. Don't fool yourself. So, he's called you. That doesn't mean anything. He's probably just doing it to ease his conscience.'

Sheryl knew it was no use contradicting Amy. The best thing to do was to listen to Amy and let her get out whatever emotions she was feeling in that moment. It wasn't the first time she'd picked up the phone to hear Amy in this state. In fact, it was becoming a bit of a habit. One minute, Amy was head over heels in love with Jason and the next, she was screaming down the phone telling Sheryl how much she hated him. And although Sheryl loved her friend to bits, she had to side with Jason on this one. He'd been stuck at home, terrified, not knowing what had happened to his girlfriend and meanwhile, Amy was digging a hole so deep, there may not be a way back. Sheryl knew her friend and she knew that when she was this erratic, it was because she had done something. She'd done something she couldn't remember and rather than deal with the problem, she was busy trying to punish the innocent party. *Am I really siding with Jason?* She almost didn't recognise herself.

Sheryl tried her best to calm Amy down. That was all she could do for now. It wasn't the right time to start singing Jason's praises. That would only anger Amy more. She was irrational as it was.

'Listen, lovely. You have got to calm down. Remember what your therapist said to you? Every time you feel this way and every time you can't remember, it's important to stay as calm as you can. Getting yourself into this state won't solve anything. It can only make it all worse. And that's not what you need right now. So, calm yourself down. Take a deep breath and then take another one. I'll call you back in a few minutes to see how you're doing. Keep your phone on you, OK?'

'OK…'

'I'll handle Jason for now. I'll just tell him you're safe, nothing else. That's all he needs to know right now. Jeez, Amy, he's doing his nut in. Meanwhile, go have a shower, get changed and make something hot. Oh, and don't go near any alcohol. You hear me?'

'OK…'

'We'll talk again in a few minutes. See you then, sweetie.'

Sheryl put down the phone. What was she going to do about Jason? It wasn't looking good. The situation was bad, really bad. Sheryl couldn't face Jason right now. Her priority was Amy. She sent him a text and thought it best to be vague for now. *Jason, sorry I missed your call. I've just heard from Amy. She's safe. I don't know any more just yet. I'll be in touch soon. S x'*

She put down the phone and sighed. She was worried about Amy, really worried. It wasn't the first time Amy had done this. She'd blacked out before. Every time this did happen, every time Amy did have a blackout, there were consequences. Sheryl didn't have a choice. She had to get involved. She felt responsible for Amy. She always had done. Amy was only fifteen when she left home and came to stay with Sheryl and her family. And since that moment, the moment where Sheryl had invited Amy into her home, she had taken her on, almost as her own. She called herself the sister Amy had never had. It was Sheryl's job to protect her no matter what. And if that meant another series of sleepless nights and interventions, she was prepared to go there.

She picked up her phone and dialled Amy's number. No answer. 'Come on, Amy. Work with me here.'

Jason opened the message from Sheryl. 'Finally!' Jason knew that if anyone knew something, it was Sheryl. Sheryl always knew where Amy was. Jason had contacted anyone and everyone else before calling Sheryl when he knew he should've just called her in the first place.

'Jason, sorry I missed your call. I've just heard from Amy. She's safe. I don't know any more just yet. I'll be in touch soon. S x'

He knew it was bad. Sheryl was never that nice on text and that was saying something. And anyway, if she'd heard from Amy, she obviously knew more than she was letting on. If he knew anything about Sheryl, it was that she was a terrible liar. Always had been. That was probably why she'd texted instead of calling. Should he call her back? Probably not. Not just yet anyway. He was going out of his mind with worry. He hadn't heard from his own girlfriend in ages and her best friend wasn't giving anything away.

He remembered the last time this had happened. He'd waited ages to hear back from her and when he had, he was left feeling shattered. They'd almost broken up. They'd rowed for days. Amy hadn't been ready to see Jason straight away. She'd made up some crap about needing space. He'd almost felt like she'd turned the tables on him. But he loved her. He loved her so much more than he hated her in that moment. So, he'd agreed to give her some space before speaking. Of course, superwoman had been the one to mediate. She always did. Sometimes, he felt like he was speaking to Amy through plate glass, Sheryl being that glass.

Once they'd finally spoken, he knew there was something Amy wasn't telling him. To this day, she swore it was because she didn't know what to tell him. She didn't remember anything.

She'd blacked out. She knew she shouldn't drink. She knew this was what alcohol did to her. And that was how desperate she'd been. Was this somehow his fault? His mind couldn't help but wonder. He couldn't help but think back to the night they'd met and just how easy it had been to get Amy into bed. He hated thinking this way, especially now, now that he'd fallen for her, fallen so hard. But he had to be honest with himself. He knew she was hiding something, whether she knew it or not.

And then the weeks had passed and she'd come crying, begging for him to take her back. She hadn't meant to be so distant and cold. She was completely overwhelmed. She'd even brought her parents and her childhood into it. He knew how much they'd messed her up. She would do anything, even go back to therapy if that was what he wanted. All she needed was to be his girlfriend again. Nothing else mattered, just him, just them.

Of course, he'd taken her back. How could he not? She was the only woman for him. In those past weeks, he'd got offers. He wasn't denying that. His mates had even tried to set him up a couple of times, but he wasn't interested. All he wanted was Amy and deep down, he knew that Amy was aware of this.

That was how they'd got back together. Slowly, they'd found their way back to each other. Amy had even gone back to therapy. She was doing it all for him. He wanted her to do it for herself. It was no good getting better for him. Amy needed to go back to therapy for the right reasons. He didn't have the heart to stop her though. If that was her goal, he was OK with it for now. The conversation could wait.

Amy had even cut out drinking for a while. She'd stopped alcohol altogether. One glass could only lead to another. Amy was finally taking control of her life.

Jason would never know what happened that night, and to

this very day, Amy swore she didn't either. Jason had chosen to believe her. The alternative just didn't bear thinking about. He'd chosen to believe her but had made her promise she would never scare him like this again. She promised. She promised she would never again do anything to jeopardise their relationship. From now on, it was just the two of them, and Sheryl occasionally, but he could cope with that.

Except it wasn't, was it? She'd let him down again, big time. This time, he didn't know if he could forgive her. He didn't know if he could go through all that again. He knew she'd done something serious. He could feel it in his gut. He picked up a glass and threw it against the wall. It smashed into pieces, just like his heart. She'd broken his heart yet again, and this time there was no coming back from it.

Amy must've had at least ten missed calls, all from Sheryl. She'd done everything Sheryl had said. She'd had a shower. She'd got changed. She was about to sit down with a cup of tea. Nobody had knocked for ages. Amy felt calmer.

The phone went again. She knew she had to answer this time.

'Where were you? Are you OK? I've been going out of my mind here.'

'Sorry… I've just sat down. I did everything you said.' Amy felt like an obedient child.

'Right. So, time to have a proper chat.' Sheryl got into teacher mode. 'What happened to you last night? And don't even think about keeping any secrets from me or forgetting any details. We went through that last time. I'm your friend. I'm here to help you, not judge you. So, talk to me, and don't leave anything out.'

'Oh, Sheryl. I'm sorry. I've done this to you again. You don't deserve this. You don't deserve to be wasting your day running around after me. I'm so sorry.'

'Never mind that, Amy. You can apologise later. Jason's been going out of his mind and to be honest, so have I. I know what you said earlier, but he loves you. He really does. And this is me saying it – Sheryl! The one who was against you guys getting together in the first place, remember? I gave him such a hard time for so long. He had to earn my trust. But he really loves you Ames, and I mean that. Please tell me you haven't done anything to jeopardise that. Please…'

'I can't, Sheryl. I wish I could but I can't.'

'So, you mean…?' Sheryl was dreading the reply.

'I think so…'

'Oh, Amy. What have you done? Don't you remember what happened last time? You had to have a termination, for goodness' sake. You had to avoid Jason for weeks. You had to lie to his face. Heck, I had to lie to his face. And to this day, he still thinks you don't know what happened.'

'I know, Sheryl.' Amy was crying now.

'You promised me you wouldn't do this. You promised you'd call me and we'd find a way. We said we'd talk about things. You promised!' Sheryl was furious now. She could feel the anger mounting. She couldn't help it. Not only had Amy gone back on her promises, she'd done it yet again. She'd put herself in an unforgivable position.

'Don't shout at me, Sheryl, please! You don't think I know what I've done? You don't think I know I've been stupid? I've broken the one promise I made to the person that means the most to me.' Amy couldn't believe that Sheryl was turning against her. Why was Sheryl speaking to Amy like this when she needed her the most? Did she think this would help? Well, she was wrong. It wasn't helping. If anything, it was making everything worse.

'I'm so angry, Amy. I don't wanna be but I am. Do you even realise what you've done? You know how you get when you drink. You know you black out. Even the doctors have told you this. We all have. So why do it anyway? For what? A meaningless night out? What was it, Amy? Come on!'

'I can't talk to you when you're like this!' Amy almost hung up the phone.

'When I'm like this? Are you serious? Like what, Amy? Is it because you're hearing a few home truths? Is that making you feel just a little bit uncomfortable?' Amy had to be told. Sheryl knew she wouldn't like it but this was no time to be catering to Amy's ego.

'Stop it! Stop it!' Amy screamed down the phone. She'd never screamed at Sheryl before but this time she couldn't control herself. Sheryl had pressed a few buttons and it was just too much for Amy to bear.

'I can't keep protecting you like this, Amy. I just can't. It's exhausting. Don't you realise that? You're twenty-seven and you're living the life of an eighteen year-old, a reckless one at that. You have got to get your act together and stop all this crap. We can't keep going down this road. I can't keep doing this.' Sheryl's voice suddenly started to crack. The exhaustion could be heard a mile off. Sadly though, she knew Amy wouldn't see her side. All she would hear was the anger in Sheryl's voice. And Amy would begrudge her this for weeks to come.

Sheryl took a breath and waited for Amy to say something, anything. She didn't. They stayed quiet for the next few minutes and then Amy was gone. Sheryl put down the phone and wept.

Now that Jason knew Amy was safe, he should've felt a sense of relief. But if anything, he was angry. He was very angry. He went to the kitchen and got out the brandy. He knew this wouldn't solve anything, but then he also knew that there was no way to solve the situation, not this time. It was over this time. It was over and Jason couldn't think of anything better to do than to drink his problems away.

'To you, Amy!' He raised his glass and took his first sip. He was on dangerous ground. Alcohol wasn't his friend, especially when he was drinking for all the wrong reasons. But what else was there to do? What else could he do?

After about three glasses, he was starting to feel much braver. The worry he'd felt for his beloved Amy was beginning to subside. It was being replaced with feelings of madness and fury. The rage was mounting and all the love and fear he'd been left with less than an hour ago was quickly disappearing.

Amy should hear this. She deserved to be a part of this moment. The realisation he was having felt almost refreshing, so did the brandy. He knew he wouldn't be saying this in a few hours but at this moment in time, it was about the here and now. Forget the future; forget tomorrow. Amy obviously had. She obviously didn't care about him. Sheryl had all but said it in her message. He wasn't stupid. There was a reason he hadn't heard from Amy and an even better reason he had from Sheryl. He'd been blindsided once again. Last time had been bad enough. There was no need to go back there. He'd taken her back and she'd sworn she would never do anything like this again.

'Enough!' he screamed. 'Enough now!' His rage was pouring out like a volcano that had been dormant for far too long and he was feeling braver than ever. He knew the feeling of victory wouldn't last. In a few hours, he would feel like absolute crap. But forget the future. He poured himself another glass.

'Amy, it's time for you to finally experience the pain I've

been going through. No more walking on eggshells. I've been doing that for far too long.' He raised his glass to her again, almost as if she was in the room. He walked across the living room and as he went to sit down, he heard his phone go off. That could only be one person. He had a special ringtone for her.

'Sheryl, hi! It's been a while! Great to hear from you.' He couldn't have sounded any more enthusiastic if he'd tried. He took another sip to check he wasn't dreaming. His girlfriend's BFF was about to break the news for her coward of a friend. He couldn't wait to hear this one.

'Jason, are you OK? Have you been drinking?'

'Got it in one, Sheryl! You always were a clever cookie. I knew there was a reason I liked you.' Jason sipped more brandy. *And they say men can't multitask. Women say a lot of things, don't they?*

'Jason, listen. I need to talk to you.'

'Go ahead, hun. I'm all ears. I can't wait to hear this one. What's she done this time? Has she fallen off a building? Is that why she can't open the door or pick up the bloody phone herself? Is she paying you to keep doing this, Sheryl? Super Sheryl, to the rescue! You really are a trooper, Sheryl. Give me a minute. I need more brandy. Let's toast to you. Hang on while I multitask here. There we are. And women say men can't! Women say a lot of things, don't they though, Sheryl? They make promises. They make you fall for them, don't they? I mean really fall for them! And then, just to make sure you can't fall any harder, they go and stomp on your heart. So go on then, Sheryl. Tell me I'm wrong. Tell me Amy's tucked up in bed. Tell me she's sick with the flu.'

'Jason, listen…'

'Go on, Sheryl. Don't spare my feelings. Tell me Amy hasn't cheated on me again. Tell me she hasn't gone out and met someone else. I can take it. Me and my friend *Brandy* here are having a great time.'

'Jason…'

'Amy thought she was so slick last time. Did she really think I was that stupid? Did she really think I wouldn't figure out what was going on? She stayed away for ages. She made me feel like it was my fault. I actually felt guilty, Sheryl! Me! When all I've done since we've been together is be faithful.'

'Jason, she had no choice but to terminate…'

'Terminate? Terminate? Wait, are you telling me Amy terminated what could have been my baby? Better still, are you telling me she got herself pregnant and didn't know who the daddy was?' His voice was cracking.

'But, Jason, you just said you knew… Oh God, what have I done? I'm so sorry, Jason.'

'Sorry? You're sorry? Why are you sorry, Sheryl? What do you have to be sorry about? No, no. Our dear Amy should be the one to apologise. I can't thank her enough for ruining my life. It's happened again, hasn't it? She's cheated.'

'I'm not sure, Jason…'

'Don't worry, Sheryl. You don't need to answer that one. We both know the answer already. Listen, I don't wanna be rude but I can't do this right now. I've gotta go.'

Jason was a broken man. He didn't think he could ever come back from this one. And if he never saw Amy again, it would be too soon. She'd finally managed it. She'd broken him.

Sheryl couldn't believe what she'd just done. There are secrets in life you just don't share, especially when you're talking about your best friend. It doesn't matter if you've just argued. 'Come on, Sheryl!' But he seemed to know what she was talking about.

He said he knew. He sounded so convincing. What had she just done? She'd just given away her best friend's biggest secret and completely ruined any chance they had of ever getting back together.

OK, think about it. They were never actually going to get back together, were they? But hang on, how do you know this for certain? How can you be sure they can't get past this? They got through it last time, didn't they? He forgave her. He forgave her even though he knew she'd slept with someone else. So, all this time he's known and hasn't said anything? All this time? And Amy didn't pick up on it. She didn't pick up on anything. She thought she had the upper hand, as usual. She always thinks she's one step ahead. She always thinks she has everything under control. She spends her time controlling everything and everyone around her. All this time, I've taken her side. All this time, I've blamed him for every little thing that went wrong in their relationship. But all the while, he was carrying this. He knew.

Sheryl couldn't believe she hadn't seen it before. She'd been so blinded by her friendship with Amy, she never let herself see Amy for who she really was. Amy constantly thought she could wrap people around her little finger. She always thought that if she turned on the water works, Sheryl would come running and Sheryl did, every time. No wonder Amy was the way she was. No wonder she always got her way. For a moment, Sheryl stopped feeling guilty. Just for a moment.

She did have one thing left to do. She had to let Amy know she'd let her secret slip. She had to tell her before Amy heard it from Jason. The mood Jason was in, Sheryl didn't know what he was capable of, not that she blamed him. This time, she didn't blame him. This time, she understood. She understood Jason's pain. She understood why sometimes, he was short with her, short with Amy even. She understood why they would argue. Jason had his reasons.

All this time, Sheryl had been protecting Amy when really, she should've stayed out of it. She didn't know the truth. She didn't know anything. Who was she to meddle in other people's relationships?

It was time to ring Amy and tell her the truth. She was prepared to face the consequences. She felt guilty about what she'd done but if she was honest with herself, a little part of her was also relieved. Today was the day she was finally letting go of all the responsibility she'd taken on. Amy was selfish and irresponsible, and it was time to grow up.

Sheryl picked up the phone and waited for the call to connect.

Amy saw yet another missed call from Sheryl. Wasn't she getting the message? Amy wasn't in the mood to speak to her right now. She was hurt and upset. Sheryl should've known that. Sheryl should've known Amy was vulnerable right now but instead, she was too busy attacking her. How dare she!

No, she wasn't going to give anyone the satisfaction. If Sheryl wanted to speak to her, she could leave a message. That was what the answering machine was there for, after all.

Amy was so frustrated. She was so over being treated like a child. Sheryl had always been that way. She just loved taking on the role of her mother and Amy let her. The truth was that when she was younger, she probably needed it. And then somehow, they got into a habit. Sheryl was always right and Amy listened to whatever Sheryl told her. Well, not anymore. It was time to make a serious change. Their argument had obviously happened for a reason. She couldn't get over the fact that Sheryl had turned on her in such a way.

The phone pinged and brought Amy right back to reality. She clicked onto the voice message. Sheryl had left a long one.

'Amy, hi, it's me. I know you're probably busy or you're just not ready to speak to me. That's fine. Before, I think I would've reacted very differently. I probably would've kept calling until you answered. But I think that today, we've said all there is to say. I know you felt attacked earlier and I get that. I lost my temper with you and for that I'm sorry. But you have to see things from my perspective. I know you're probably rolling your eyes right about now. It's not easy always trying to pick up after your mess, especially when you only want my help on your terms. I've really tried to be a good friend to you, and I'd like to think that I have been. Whenever you've needed me, I've been there, or at least I've tried to be. But, Amy, where are you when I need you? Did you even stop to think about why I reacted this way today? Don't you know what day it is? No, I suspect not. I'm not upset, Amy, just disappointed I guess. After all these years of friendship, you see fit to throw it away because of a mistake you've made. I'm sorry to say it this way but it's true. And I think deep down, you remember more than you're letting on. The truth is you have hurt the people around you, the only people who have ever truly cared about you. Not just me but Jason. You've really hurt him, Amy.

'Anyway, that's the other reason I was calling. Jason knows. He knows everything. He's known all this time, Amy. He knows that you were with another man that night and he suspects that last night was a repeat performance.

'I have a confession to make. He knows about the baby too. I'm really sorry. Jason was telling me he knew and I let it slip thinking he was talking about the baby. From the bottom of my

161

heart, I'm sorry for that, Amy. I know you're going to think it was done on purpose to get revenge, but it really wasn't. To be honest, Jason needed to know the truth. You know that as well as I do. He's known about this other man for ages and he's stuck by you. What does that say to you, Amy? It should tell you everything you need to know.

'I don't know if it's too late for you both but I wanted to give you a heads up and tell you the truth. I won't bother you after this. The truth is, I think we need some space. You have some serious thinking to do and I'm just exhausted. I'm not saying we can't still be friends. I guess I'm just saying I need to stop meddling in your relationship so much and let you get on with your life, just like I know you want. Call him, Amy, or go round. Show him you still care. He deserves that much at least. Bye, Amy.'

Amy was stunned. Was Sheryl giving up on her? Was she losing her only real friend in the world? Without even realising it, she started crying. Who was she kidding? She couldn't cope without Sheryl. She hated to admit it but it was true. Sheryl had always been there, always. And Amy had never thought about what life would be like without her. She had a feeling she was about to find out.

It took Amy a moment to register the rest of the message and realise what Sheryl had just confessed. Jason knew about the baby. He knew about everything. She desperately wanted to be angry at Sheryl, angry that Sheryl had told Jason, but she couldn't bring herself to be. She knew that Sheryl was right. She knew that she hadn't intentionally let the truth slip. Five minutes ago, Amy would've wanted to kill Sheryl for doing this to her. Yet now, knowing that she may just have lost her best friend, her only friend, forever, she didn't feel any anger. Just sadness.

She was at a loss. All her defences were down. She didn't recognise herself. In the last twenty-four hours, she'd gone through a whirlwind of emotions. She didn't know what was real anymore. She realised she had to find a way to pull herself together. What was the point otherwise? She knew deep down that she'd got herself into this mess. Sheryl was right. Only she was to blame.

Without thinking, she picked up her car keys and rushed out the door. She didn't think to change. She didn't think to check the state of her face. She had to speak to Jason. She had to speak to him now. She had to find a way to explain in the hope that maybe, just maybe he would hear her out.

She drove frantically, knowing she would probably get a fine or two in the morning. But hey, life couldn't possibly get any worse right now, so what the hell!

It was only when she reached Jason's driveway that she stopped to think about what she was doing. What if he didn't want to see her? What if she was making a big mistake? What then?

She didn't know what to do. She sat in her car, hoping the answer would come to her, all the while knowing it wouldn't.

Get out of the car. Come on! Amy still had her key to the place. Using it would be a risk but not using it would be an even greater one. She walked over to the door, slowly, all the while weighing her options. She turned the key in the door and quietly stepped in. Immediately, she noticed Sheryl's coat. What was Sheryl doing at Jason's place? What was she even doing there? Amy was terrified of what she was about to discover. Surely Sheryl had just come round to check on Jason. Surely that was all she was about to find.

Amy never stuck around to find out. Little did she know that when Sheryl had got to Jason's place, she'd found him unconscious. Amy would never listen to Sheryl's next message telling her Jason had ended up in intensive care from alcohol poisoning.

That day, Amy had walked away. She had walked away thinking that Jason and Sheryl had done the unimaginable. She hadn't considered that this wasn't the case. Her mind had wandered to places she never knew existed. Jason and Sheryl… The two people that mattered most to her in the world.

Amy would never answer Sheryl's call. She wasn't Jason's next of kin so she wouldn't be told about his condition. Amy had no idea what she would do next. She was about to walk away from the only life that she had ever known.

Loose Ends

Amanda had been waiting eagerly by the phone for the last hour. She felt like she had been summoned to court and had been told the jury had come to their final decision. She must've checked about twenty times that the phone was still plugged in. Her mobile was on full blast so there was no way she could miss this life-changing call, even if she tried.

Amanda had been dreaming of this moment for years. She had put all her hopes on this process. It certainly hadn't been an easy one. Eighteen months of forms, questions, visits. Countless cleaning sprees to make damn sure that every corner of her flat was spotless. Amanda had known that anything could go wrong at any given moment and there was no way she was going to let that happen. She had been so determined to make it all work. She had given up her life, sacrificed her career, her love life even. Her love life wasn't really going anywhere anyway, so maybe that one didn't quite count.

Amanda sat and waited. Perhaps another cup of tea would calm her down. She'd had five already in the last three hours. Nerves were definitely getting the better of her today. She'd been up since five, checking the paperwork, cleaning the flat again and rushing around like there was no tomorrow.

It was now two o'clock and the phone hadn't rung. The agency had promised to call before one thirty. So why hadn't they? She knew that companies never stuck to their promised time but she lived in the hope like the rest of the nation that just once, she could be proven wrong on this one.

Who was she kidding? Of course, they weren't going to call when they said they would. Of course, they weren't going to honour their promise. They hadn't made a promise to begin with. Yet she took it as a promise, because this was a life we were talking about, and not just hers. Somebody else's. A life that she hoped to share her own with from now.

She had said a prayer last night. She wasn't really very religious at all. She never had been. But she hoped to be heard this time. Just this once, she hoped that her lucky star could protect her and honour her wishes. She knew she wasn't supposed to ask. That wasn't what prayers were for really, but she couldn't help herself. She wanted this so much. She hadn't known until just a few years ago how much she wanted this, but she was certain now. Just as well, as her thirty-fifth birthday was coming up next month. It was time she knew what she wanted out of her life, the only life she would have. She could still hear her mother now. 'You only live once, so make the most of it, Amanda!' She had made this her motto since her mother's death seven years ago.

Her mother had been a strong woman. Before her accident, she had worked and taken care of Amanda as a single mum. She had gone to great lengths to ensure that her only daughter could receive a private education. It hadn't been easy but Amanda's mum was a determined woman who didn't take no for an answer. If she wanted something, she went for it. Amanda had grown up looking up to her mum. In her eyes, her mum was as tough as *Wonder Woman* or *Superwoman*, or well, both put together.

When her dad left them, Amanda was only five. She wasn't old enough to understand what this meant. For years, she had been made to believe that he was away and that one day, he might come back. Her mother couldn't break her daughter's heart the way her father had broken her own. So, she lied. She lied in the hope that when Amanda did eventually realise he wasn't coming back, she'd be strong enough to cope. And maybe deep down, her mum hoped he might one day come through those doors, begging her to take him back. But this wasn't *EastEnders*. They both knew he never would. So, from then onwards, Amanda's mother had been a mum and dad rolled into one and she had done a wonderful job of taking care of her daughter until Amanda turned eighteen. This was until the day her mum was involved in a car accident leaving her severely disabled, a day which had changed everything. It took her a while to get used to the life which was so suddenly forced upon them both.

From that moment, Amanda effectively put her own life on hold. She decided to go for a course at The Open University, as leaving for university wasn't an option at the time. But she just wasn't able to keep up with the course. Money was too tight and Amanda split her time between work and caring for her mum instead. She was so grateful the day she joined a group of carers at the local community centre. Meanwhile, someone from the local support group would come round and look after her mum.

She really looked forward to these meetings, even if the same couldn't quite be said for her mother. Everyone was just lovely. She never thought that at the age of twenty, she would appreciate a tea and biscuit this much! That was where she ended up meeting the person who would become one of her closest friends, Jane. Poor Jane was going through a tough time. Her dad had only just been diagnosed with early-onset Alzheimer's disease, and she was adjusting to life as a new carer. Jane was quite the businesswoman, so the change hit her hard at first.

Amanda and Jane ended up getting very close, and Jane was

167

really there for Amanda after her mum's death. Her poor father ended up in hospital two years after Amanda lost her mum. They just hadn't been able to cope towards the end. It was such a dreadful illness. At least Amanda's mum was still able to communicate until her last moments. But Jane's father, well, he had stopped communicating altogether.

Jane would probably be coming round in the next week or so. Now that she was engaged to Eric, Amanda didn't see much of her. That was not to say they didn't keep in touch. Hours of phone conversations were proof of that. It was just one of those things. Life went on, didn't it?

Amanda was getting very impatient. Maybe she should call the agency. She was just dying to know if she was going to be a mum! There was only one way to find out. The agency would call, eventually. At least she hoped so.

Amanda just couldn't take it anymore. Her nerves were getting the best of her and no matter how hard she tried to keep herself busy, she just couldn't help but worry.

The process had really taken its toll, especially when they had asked her about her decision to adopt as a single mum. This tended to make the process more complicated because the adoption agency needed to make sure that the child in question would be cared for in a stable, loving family. They usually preferred a loving family of three, with both parents involved. But then, they'd never met Amanda's mother!

Yet Amanda had put her life on hold for so long that when it came to meeting men, it just didn't tend to turn into a long-term relationship. Amanda was a pro at dates. She did all the right things to impress from her dress sense to her sense of humour to her willingness to pay half the bill. But then came the follow-up dates which didn't go quite as smoothly. Men never really wanted to commit, or better yet, they were often attached. They were very good at hiding that one at first. But after a while, Amanda became better at spotting serial datists who weren't quite as single as they professed to be on the first date.

There had been this one guy, Jason. He was just gorgeous. Amanda ended up falling for him pretty much straight away. She'd met him a year after her mum's passing. She was in a strange place, vulnerable. She didn't know if she was quite ready for a relationship, but she found herself feeling very lonely. Jane had been the one to encourage her to go out and start meeting new people. She almost went as far as to post her on a couple of dating sites. But that was a no-no on Amanda's part and for the sake of their friendship, Jane gave in.

Amanda met Jason at Sainsbury's of all places in the alcohol section. He was picking out wine. She made a joke about how French wines were all the rage, and he ended up asking her if she wanted to prove this theory to him over a glass of Chablis at his. Amanda never usually accepted such invitations. She was always very cautious. They would meet in a bar, or a pub, or some restaurant she never knew the name of. But somehow, she found herself completely charmed by Jason. So, they headed over to his, and over a bottle, they poured their hearts out to each other.

Poor Jason had been in hospital for over a month. He hadn't wanted to go into too much detail but Amanda could see he wasn't in a good place. She didn't have to know Jason well to work that one out. He hadn't made any advances or asked to show her his bedroom. In fact, he was the first man to call her a taxi and phone to check she'd made it home safely. She wasn't saying she was irresistible or anything. Well, she was. But for him to be the perfect gentleman, she had to wonder what had happened to him to make him so cautious.

That night, she'd been on the phone to Jane for at least an hour. After all that, did love at first sight exist? She'd never thought so up until that evening. Now, she wondered whether she'd been wrong about that one. Was she in love? Or was it the wine? Chablis certainly did the trick! She'd be adding that to her shopping list from now on.

They ended up meeting up at least once a week. They made a point of trying all the Waitrose and Sainsbury's wines they could get their hands on. They took turns in choosing a bottle and their evenings together became her favourites.

Yet Amanda quickly sensed they were entering the friend zone. She was kicking herself at first, but a few weeks into their dates, if you could call them that, Jason started to confide in Amanda. The woman he'd fallen for had hurt him in ways he didn't know existed. He'd never met anyone like her. He wasn't someone who fell easily, but he had fallen under her spell from the get-go. It turned out there was a time where he was quite the womaniser. She knew it!

When Amanda found out that Jason had been cheated on not once but twice and that the woman of his dreams had aborted a baby he wasn't even sure was his without telling him, she knew that things between them were not about to go any further. He was still very much in love with this woman. What a lucky lady she was! And she didn't even know it. Amanda couldn't stand this woman she'd never met!

After Jason, Amanda hadn't met anyone worth giving up her life for. So instead, she'd decided that being single was the right step for her. After all, she'd always been told that love usually appeared in someone's life when they were least looking for it, so if in fact this was true, the last thing she wanted to do was chase after a non-existent love of her life.

She'd been very honest with the adoption agency and the case worker in particular. She'd also explained in some detail that she herself had grown up in a one parent household with her mother. It had never done her any harm. If anything, it had empowered her both as a woman and a mother-to-be. Her idol and inspiration had been her mother from the get-go and she wanted to do the same for a little angel out there. The case worker had sympathised with her and had explained that whilst this wasn't an ideal situation, she would do everything she could to support Amanda. Amanda couldn't ask for more.

2.15 p.m. and still no call. Was this a bad sign? Amanda hoped more than anything that it wasn't. She had learnt to manifest what she wanted most in life. So, to keep herself going, she manifested like never before in the hope that the agency would call and make her one dream come true.

Both Jason and Jane had texted practically every hour on the dot. Still nothing though, which was driving Amanda completely insane. It was strange how days could go by without people noticing them, yet if you were expecting something, time seemed to come to a standstill. It was almost unbearable.

It had taken over a year to get to this point even though countless children were in care homes. It just made no sense to Amanda who at the start was naive enough to believe that financial stability would be enough to convince the agency that she deserved a child. She soon learned how mistaken she was.

There had been so many questions about her financial situation. This was one aspect of the process she didn't mind. Years ago, when she was still caring for her mum, she worked for minimum wage. Her objective was to get a job and support herself and her mum as well as she could, even if it meant going without any extras for a while. But after her mum's passing, Jane convinced Amanda to go back to her studies and get an education. Amanda was reluctant to begin with. She would be a mature student and wasn't sure if she had the confidence to succeed in a world she didn't feel she belonged to. But when Amanda started her business course at the local college, eventually leading to a university degree, she found that she was more able than she had thought possible.

During the day, she worked and evenings, she studied. She didn't have anyone to come home to so she made this a priority. She knew she would be making her mum proud. This was all her mum had ever wanted for her daughter and truth be told, she was more than glad to be honouring her mum's wishes now she could. She just wished her mum could've been alive to see it.

Her course eventually led to a start-up, an online business which was slow to begin with, especially as Amanda found it so hard to find investors. How grateful she was to Eric, Jane's boyfriend at the time, for believing in her. He had become so successful in his field that he could afford to put money aside. She was so proud of being able to pay back every penny a few years later, with interest.

Amanda was now in a position to work from home and care for a child of her own. It was ironic that years earlier, she had cared for her mum. The only difference was that now, she was earning over three times as much.

The case worker had confirmed that if she was as financially stable as she promised, this was in fact a great advantage and would speed up the adoption process. If only this had been the case.

Amanda understood that the agency had to complete checks

before taking her application forward. She had no problem waiting for this part of the process to be completed as she was confident that what she had to offer was more than good enough. In some ways, it felt like a business transaction. She had become so used to these.

Amanda wondered what could be taking so long. She had no way of knowing whether this was a good or bad sign. She was someone who often doubted herself and sometimes tended to see the glass half empty. She was trying hard not to do this where the adoption was concerned, but it was hard.

All she could do was wait. Jason and Jane had both told her to ring them if she needed anything, but she was too nervous to pick up the phone. What if she missed the call? What if she was on the phone when her case worker was trying to get in touch with her? Would the agency then decide she wasn't fit to be a parent if she missed their call? She was driving herself mad, desperately hoping to hear something soon.

Amanda sat by the phone, praying to her mum this time, hoping for some kind of miracle. She knew her mum would listen one way or the other. She just hoped that her mum would help her become a parent in the next few hours. No, not hours, minutes!

It was nearly four o'clock. What was taking her case worker so long? She wished she had told her friends to come over now. They'd even asked if she wanted them to take the day off. But in her mind, it was best if she was alone when taking the call. If it was good news, she could shout and scream like a maniac, and if it was bad news, she could sob to her heart's content with a good bottle of Chablis, without having to share this time. Amanda could only hope that the news she was about to receive was good news.

In her initial interview with the adoption agency, before being assigned a case worker, she remembered being asked why she had chosen to adopt. So many prospective parents chose this route after discovering they couldn't have children of their own. This was often a last resort, which was not to say that they were choosing to adopt for the wrong reasons. So often though, people hoped to become parents naturally and finding out they couldn't conceive was devastating.

Amanda's reasons were different. They were personal. Her mum had always told her there were too many lonely children in the world as it was. So many people had children without even giving it a second thought. In the UK alone, poverty, abuse, neglect and countless other serious issues were reasons why so many parents struggled and so many children ended up in the system. As a solicitor, she so often found herself helping mothers and fathers fight for the custody of their children, even though in her own personal view, they didn't always deserve the opportunity. Yet her mother knew that her job was not to express an opinion, but to defend the cases that she had taken on, even if sometimes, she didn't believe in her clients. Her mother was a determined woman, so nine times out of ten, she would help her clients get their children back.

Amanda knew her mother would be proud to see her trying to rescue one of these children, whom she always considered to be the greatest victims of all. Children didn't ask to be born, so when they were mistreated by people who didn't deserve to be their parents, her mother was secretly furious. And over time, this made her daughter just as angry.

Yet Amanda had another reason which she shared with her case worker later in the process. They had become quite friendly at this point and she felt like she could almost call the woman a friend, though she had to bear in mind that the decision could still go against her at any moment.

Years ago, Amanda had known a girl she'd been to school with. She was still haunted now by the tragedy which had occurred at her school on that fateful day. Amanda and this girl often crossed paths in the corridor. Amanda's locker was only about two lockers away from hers. Whenever Amanda saw this girl, she looked forlorn, lost somehow. Amanda wasn't in her class or anything. In fact, she was a year below this girl. But she knew just like everyone else in the school that she was being bullied. She knew the situation was bad. Amanda still hated herself now for ignoring the signs. Her mother had always taught her to be a fighter, but Amanda hadn't fought. She hadn't stopped it. She hadn't even tried. She hadn't ever done anything directly to her, but she had never tried to intervene either. When the case worker asked her why, Amanda admitted that she was scared. She knew that if someone was being bullied and you tried to take their side, you would eventually be on the receiving end yourself. And Amanda was just too afraid of this happening. She wasn't making excuses for herself, even though maybe deep down, she was trying to ease her guilt.

Amanda remembered the last time she saw her in the corridor. The girl carried a sad smile, almost like she was both terrified and relieved at the same time. Amanda didn't know what this meant at the time. She was young and naive. Or maybe just ignorant. But when later she went to the toilet to wash her hands before lunch, she noticed tablets all over the floor. The door was locked and in a moment of panic, Amanda ran out and looked for the nearest adult she could find. The girl had taken her own life and like so many other students in the school, Amanda had done nothing to stop it. Like so many others, Amanda was guilty. The girl's name was Lauren.

Did this make Amanda complicit to what had gone on? Was she somehow also to blame for not speaking to Lauren? Or speaking out? These were questions which haunted Amanda to this very day. She was so ashamed and carried so much guilt with her. She knew she could never do anything to make it right.

Amanda tried counselling but it never really helped ease her conscience. She decided that although she could never save Lauren from herself or others, she could try to save another child. She hadn't made this decision purely out of guilt. Of course she hadn't. But that day stayed with her nevertheless and she knew that she could only truly redeem herself by trying to do good in a world which carried so much evil in it.

Just a few days ago, Amanda had visited Lauren's grave. They had never been friends in life, but Lauren's death had somehow changed Amanda and had made her want to reach out.

Today, Amanda was hoping that her own lucky star would reach out to her and help her to make the world a better place, however small her contribution seemed in the grand scheme of things.

It was almost four thirty and Amanda still hadn't heard anything. What was it going to take for her phone to ring? There were only so many times that she could charge her phone in the space of a day. But Amanda couldn't risk her phone turning off, especially as it had been playing up lately. Amanda was supposed to upgrade nearly six months ago, but she was a little busy sorting out the rest of her life at the time. Technology was hardly a priority.

They had promised to ring today. She had to believe that.

This wasn't an employer calling to confirm a job offer, or a GP practice calling to change an appointment. This was the adoption of a child. She thought this should make all the difference, but then everything was slow in this country, so what made this any different? Surely, she could count on her case worker not to let her down though.

Her case worker had been so genuine the whole way through. She knew how tough this process truly was. But they had to be sure that the family they were choosing for each child was the right family. They couldn't afford to make a mistake or rush into anything. The child had to be the right fit for the family and vice versa.

So many poor children had been dragged from pillar to post. There were so many terrible stories that the case worker wasn't allowed to share with Amanda. Amanda had read up on quite a few herself before applying. She had wanted to arm herself with research in order to make sure that she had every chance of adopting a child in need.

At the start of the process, Amanda was asked about her preference with regards to the child she would be adopting. Was there a specific age group? Was there a part of the world that she identified with more, or less? There was so much to think about when it came to answering those questions.

Like so many others, Amanda wished to adopt a young child. She wanted to make sure that the bond she was about to form with her child was a strong one. She knew how vital it was for mother and child to form an attachment, and she wanted more than anything to make sure that she had this opportunity.

With regards to culture or religion, she had no preference. She had always been fascinated by different cultures and languages, and she embraced this side of herself. Each culture or religion was unique and Amanda found beauty in every culture she encountered. Sadly, she knew that her views were naive and far from reality, but she had been taught to see the beauty of life, and this was her way of honouring the values that had been passed down to her, even if this wasn't the case for others.

She was asked by her case worker how she would cope if a child had been through severe trauma such as genocide, war or a cultural or religious trauma of some kind. Amanda didn't pretend to have a ready-made answer to this question, but she promised to give the child all the love and care possible, ensuring that the child's connection to his or her culture did not disappear. She would work hard to make sure that the child could experience the beauty of life that she was so desperate to share, however naive this viewpoint may seem. The case worker praised her at this point. Not everyone knew how to answer this question in particular.

Amanda was asked to look over multiple case studies to better understand what she would be dealing with should she be matched with a child who had suffered particular trauma. Interestingly, not all the case studies that Amanda was asked to study were related to minors under the age of eighteen.

One case in particular stuck with her. A young woman in her very early twenties, murdered by her father and fiancé for disrespecting the family's culture. Amanda couldn't believe what she was reading. Her best friend had given an interview in which she had clearly stated that this was in no way an accident. She strongly believed that they had meant to kill her, all in the name of honour. She would never forgive herself for not being able to save her best friend, who she believed should have been helped much earlier. She concluded by insisting that this was a clear failure in the system and that unless immediate measures were taken, these atrocities would keep happening time and time again.

Amanda was enraged at this story, all the while knowing that as a westerner, she could never fully understand certain cultural conflicts. It gave her shivers down her spine and made her more determined still to do right by at least one child.

She was intent on making a difference, however small. So, she would continue to wait by the phone if it was the last thing she ever did.

It was approaching five o'clock when the phone finally rang. Amanda thought this moment would never come, especially as she'd been waiting for the best part of the day for the phone to go off.

'Hello?' She couldn't have been more nervous if she'd tried. She did everything not to sound overly anxious. What would be would be. Oh, who was she kidding? She had never wanted anything so much in her life.

'Hi, Amanda. Listen, I'm so sorry I didn't get in touch before now. It's been a long day to say the least.' The case worker did sound slightly stressed. Maybe she was telling the truth. Or was she?

'Oh yes, of course. That's absolutely fine. I completely understand.' Amanda knew she was being too nice. Hopefully, the case worker wouldn't hear it in her voice.

'I do hope you haven't been waiting by the phone all this time. I feel just dreadful.'

'Oh, no, no. Not at all!' Amanda knew she didn't sound convincing.

'Well, Amanda. What a process it's been.' Yes, yes, Amanda knew this. She'd been part of it after all. 'We've considered your application very carefully. We've thought long and hard about what this would mean, not just for the child that you want to adopt, but for yourself.' Oh God. It really wasn't looking good, was it? 'Amanda, are you still there?'

'Oh, yes, of course.'

'Oh, good. I thought for a minute you'd stopped breathing!'

'I must admit. I'm not far off at this point!' A joke couldn't do any harm at this stage. After all, they'd made their decision.

'Oh, Amanda, I understand. Of course I do. Anyway, as I was saying, we wanted to be sure that this really was the right step for you and for us. And I'm very pleased to say that you have passed the process!'

'I'm sorry, what? Can you repeat that?'

'You've passed, Amanda. You are going to be a mum. Congratulations.' Amanda couldn't believe what she was hearing. She had passed! She had actually passed the test. She didn't know whether to laugh or to cry.

'Oh, wow! I just can't believe it. I was beginning to think it might never happen. I was preparing myself, just like you advised me to.'

'Oh, Amanda. Of course, you are going to be emotional. It's a very emotional time for you and this is completely understandable. But when reviewing your file and going through all of our conversations and interviews, I just had to push for this. There is no better person than you, Amanda. You are ready to be a mum, without a doubt.'

'I don't know what to say. Thank you. Thank you so much.' Amanda was no longer hiding her tears. Her dream was coming true, after all this time. Amanda was going to be a mum! She did her best to compose herself. She was desperate to find out what would happen next. She had been informed of this months ago, but any information had completely gone out of her mind. 'So what happens next? How long will I need to wait to…'

'Well, that's the best bit, Amanda. We've got a child for you. She's four years old. Her parents were the victims of a brutal attack and very sadly, they didn't make it.' Just like her, this little girl's life was about to change considerably. And she was only four.

'She? You mean I'm adopting a girl? A four-year-old angel? I can't believe she's lost both her parents, and in such dreadful circumstances.'

'Yes, Amanda. You are. You are adopting a little girl. I know, Amanda. It's just awful. But you'll know what to do. I believe in you.'

'Oh, wow. I just don't know what to say. I'm just speechless.'

'Of course you are. Take all the time you need to take it in. You deserve this, Amanda. You really do.' Her case worker had always been so sweet. She was perfect for the job!

'So… Who is she? Can I ask?'

'Oh, yes, of course you can. I think I'm a little overwhelmed myself. You are going to love her, Amanda. Her name is Anoush[1] and she's Armenian. She was born in the UK, and she's grown up here since. Her grand-parents came over from Turkey, after the genocide which took place in 1915.'

'Armenian? How wonderful! Does she speak the language?'

'Yes, she does. The family always spoke Armenian at home, so in some ways, Armenian is her first language.'

'Oh, this is just wonderful, wonderful news. I couldn't have hoped for more. I can promise you now. I'll make sure she continues to learn her first language alongside English. We will

---

[1] Anoush is an Armenian name meaning sweet.

embrace her culture and I'll do everything I can to make her parents proud.'

'I know you will, Amanda. That's why I was thrilled when Anoush was chosen to come to you. I just knew that you would understand her needs.'

'I can't tell you how much this means to me.'

'Oh, you don't need to. I know it does. OK, so listen, we will organise everything and Anoush will move in with you by the end of the week. And then we can take it from there. You know, Amanda, as someone who was adopted, I know just how important it is to grow up in a loving household with parents who show you the love that you need. I was so lucky myself. I didn't always realise just how fortunate I was. Anyway, what I'm trying to say is that Anoush is one lucky little girl. It'll be tough for a while for the both of you, but you'll see. As long as you're always there for her and honest with her, you will make her a very happy little girl.'

'Thank you so very much for… well, for everything.'

'No problem, Amanda. Right, I must leave you now, but see you in a couple of days. I'll be in touch before then.'

'Thank you, Claudine. I'll wait to hear from you.'

'Bye, Amanda, and congratulations once again.'

So, Claudine herself had been adopted. It made sense to Amanda. She'd always been so patient, shown extra care. Her attention to detail had impressed Amanda from the get-go and come to think of it, there were a number of questions she may never have asked Amanda had she not herself understood the complexity of adoption, both for prospective parents and the children needing a new home.

Amanda was just speechless. She couldn't believe that after all this time, it was finally happening. Her dream was coming true. She was about to become a mum!

That day had been one of the toughest for Amanda since her mum's death. She had been through a whirlwind of emotions in the hours leading up to what was to be the beginning of the rest of her life.

Claudine continued to check in regularly, especially in the first months after the adoption. She had been a great support to Amanda who now felt that she was doing everything for the first time, never quite knowing whether she was doing it right.

It took Anoush a good while to get used to her new home. For the first few weeks, she barely spoke. She didn't want to eat or drink and wouldn't go to bed without crying every night. Amanda always knew that the transition would be difficult for them both, but she had no idea it would be this tough. There were moments, especially at the start, where she found herself questioning her every move.

It was the day that Amanda started baking Armenian treats which included Khourabia and Kadaif* that Anoush smiled for the very first time. That was the day when she finally started to feel at home, even just a little. Anoush's home was evidently connected to culture, and this was what Amanda decided she would provide for her little girl. This then became a tradition for them both and their first bonding activity.

Amanda kept her promise and took Anoush to Armenian school every weekend. She found herself taking lessons and often wondered what she had got herself into, especially when her words were mispronounced and Anoush burst out laughing.

It was the day when Anoush called Amanda 'Mum' for the first time that Amanda realised just how much she loved this little

---

* Khourabia and Kadaif are sweet Armenian biscuits and desserts.

girl that had entered her life so suddenly.

Jason made a habit of coming round at least once a week. It seemed their wine tasting sessions were to be continued.

Anoush really took to Jason and the three of them became a force to be reckoned with. Having a man around really did change things for Amanda and Anoush. Amanda felt less like she was battling her way through life and Anoush just loved having a male figure around.

It had taken Jason years to realise that the woman standing in front of him had become the love of his life. He had finally fallen out of love with his ex. His feelings for Amanda were stronger than he ever imagined they could be. Funnily enough, it was over French wine that he had this realisation, Viognier this time.

Amanda never knew she could be this happy. She had spent so many years questioning whether happiness actually existed. But when she got engaged to Jason, who was willing to adopt Anoush officially, she realised she had stepped into a world completely unfamiliar to her until now.

As she started to prepare for her wedding, she thought back to all the females that had impacted her life. Her mum, Lauren, Jane, Claudine, and now her daughter, Anoush. They had all been a part of her life journey and had made her the woman she was today. Not everyone had been as lucky as Amanda, who through all her experiences and life challenges, had become a confident and empowered woman, ready for anything life could throw at her.

Her fate would be sealed the day Amanda was running late to pick up her little girl. She always made sure she was the one to pick up her daughter. Jason had offered a number of times, but

Amanda took pride in being at the gates to welcome her angel into her arms every day at three on the dot. So, when she set off later than usual, something that never happened, she panicked. To other mums, this wouldn't be a big deal, but then she wasn't like other mums. The school was good at arranging cover at the end of the day, especially if parents rang in advance. Her rational self knew that the school wouldn't mind waiting with Anoush, who had never been in any trouble before. But she wasn't feeling too rational today.

Amanda never usually used her phone in the car, but she couldn't help herself this time. She was quite the confident driver anyway so a quick conversation with the school wouldn't make a difference, if only to put her mind at ease just a little. It was true to say that Anoush and Amanda had come a very long way, but she would never forgive herself if she jeopardised that for any reason.

As she dialled, the phone fell out of her hand. Luckily, it didn't fall very far and Amanda managed to pick it up without taking her eyes off the road. She was driving slightly over the speed limit but that didn't matter. There was no CCTV in the area so she knew she could get away with it. She usually stuck to speed limits, especially since that was how her mum's accident had happened.

Amanda made the call and let the school know she was running a little late today. They were very understanding and managed to ease her guilt slightly. When she came off the phone, she heard herself breathe a huge sigh of relief. Maybe this didn't make her the worst mother in the world.

Amanda knew she wasn't paying attention to the road, and yet she could not anticipate what was just about to happen. In a moment of absence, excited at the thought of picking up her little girl, Amanda didn't stop at the red light. The junction was busy and cars were coming from all directions. She realised just a second too late that a car was coming towards her at full speed. It was too late to reverse. As Amanda froze and broke all too soon, the vehicle rammed into the passenger side and the car was dragged for what felt like miles. Amanda screamed as loud as she could, all the while knowing that she might not make it out alive.

When the vehicles eventually came to a halt after seconds of destruction and terror, Amanda lost consciousness. When she opened her eyes again, she was lying flat on the ground, unable to move. Her entire body was in excruciating pain and silent tears were streaming down her face. Amanda couldn't stay awake, which wasn't a good sign. She could hear the voices of passers-by, trying their best to keep her conscious.

When she opened her eyes a second time, Jason's eyes were gazing at hers. There was so much love in his expression. The devastation was heart-breaking.

Amanda couldn't speak. She desperately hoped that her silent thoughts could be heard by what had become her soulmate. Amanda was completely guilt-ridden. She couldn't bear to think that she was leaving the most precious little girl in the world, a girl who had lost so much already. She could feel herself drifting off and she knew she had only moments left. Jason was trying hopelessly to keep her awake, but even his love was not enough to keep his wife-to-be alive.

Amanda thought of the precious family she was leaving behind, the family she had been so proud to call her own. Nobody had helped her build it. This was all her own work. And it had been magical while it had lasted.

As Amanda continued to lose blood, she could feel the women who had shaped her life at different times calling out to her: her mum, her guardian angel; Jane, her very best friend; Claudine, her angel in disguise; and Alissia, the young woman she had never met, who had died alone at the hands of evil. And as her life flashed before her, Amanda's very last thoughts were with Lauren, the girl who had died alone, with nobody to save her. Maybe they would meet again and just maybe Lauren would forgive Amanda.

Jason glanced up for a moment, completely overwhelmed and unable to come to terms with what was happening. Before he knew it, his eyes had moved towards the car that had furiously crashed into Amanda's. The person getting out looked eerily like his ex-girlfriend and Jason could've sworn the woman he was seeing was Amy. For that one poignant moment, all the hurt, all the pain and the inconceivable betrayal that she had inflicted on him at what had been the worst point in his life flashed before his very eyes. No, it couldn't be true. It just couldn't be. All that mattered now was his beloved wife-to-be.

Amanda died in Jason's arms moments later, all the while knowing that she had received the greatest gift of all, the gift of love.

THE END